THE SPIDER:
THE EMPEROR FROM HELL

THE EMPEROR
FROM HELL

By Grant Stockbridge

POPULAR PUBLICATIONS • 2022

PUBLISHING HISTORY

"The Emperor from Hell" originally appeared in the July 1938 (Vol. 15, No. 2) issue of *The Spider* magazine. Copyright 2022 by Argosy Communications, Inc. All rights reserved.

CHAPTER 1
DUST OF DEATH

I T WAS on an October night, somber with smoky fog, that
nightmare murder, brought by a creature in the scarlet garb
of a legendary Satan, first invaded Manhattan. A puff of dust,
blown from a leathery hand with long, scarlet-tipped nails—
it was no more than that—and a man fell writhing in deathly
agony upon the floor!

To those who witnessed the murder, and there were an even
dozen, it appeared actually a thing of black magic, of demoniac sorcery. The screams of the dying man were those of a soul
tormented in hell. And when those screams were multiplied
not by tens, but by scores and hundreds—when the horror of
this mummer in scarlet strode terribly across the land, it seemed
to the trembling multitude that indeed the massacrer was the
demon he mimicked… that hell had established dominion over
a mortal and cowering earth!

It was Richard Wentworth's warmth of sympathy for his
fellow man that had made him a witness of that first portentous
death. He was at dinner in his secluded mansion behind Sutton
Place when his Hindu servitor, Ram Singh, stole silently on bare
feet up to Wentworth's shoulder.

"A man named Leary, *sahib,*" Ram Singh said softly. "A man
dismissed from the police by Kirkpatrick, *sahib.* He has information for you."

Wentworth raised his smooth black brows, smiled across at his guests—Nita van Sloan, his fiancée, and Major Randolph Dow, of the Chemical Warfare Department at Aberdeen, Maryland. Major Dow's ruddy face was turned wholly toward the

The creature of flame and scarlet scales was speaking. "Your souls are mine! When Hell speaks, you will obey!"

loveliness of Nita, but Wentworth was aware that Nita's violet eyes were fixed on himself with anxiety she could not conceal. She alone of womankind knew his every secret and to what terrible battles a mere whispered word might summon him.

"Really, Miss van Sloan," Major Dow was saying, "I'm sure I could offer you many more advantages than this chap you're engaged to. Why, look at his criminal record! Positively, I think I shall have to move to have Wentworth expelled from the Voyagers' Club." He flashed a big-toothed smile at Wentworth.

Wentworth's firmly modeled lips were curved in a faint smile as he warmed a glass of Napoleon brandy between his palms.

"Tell Leary to wait," he directed Ram Singh quietly. "Major Dow, do you think a hostile move would be... *wise*, with a man of my record?"

Dow threw up both blunt-fingered hands—scrupulously cleaned hands which nevertheless bore chemical stains. *"Kamerad!"* he cried. "I'll never mention it again—or I might turn into another unproven charge of murder against you!"

Both men were laughing, but there was fire in the violet depths of Nita van Sloan's eyes, and her voice was low and full. "I don't think that's funny at all," she said, "and if you dislike consorting with criminals, remember I have a record, too!"

Wentworth's face sobered as he regarded her. He pushed back his chair and rose, Ram Singh instantly at his side. It was the one curse of the life he had chosen, the one regret of his years of service to humanity as the secret avenger who struck at the criminal heart of the nation, that Nita should become occasionally involved. At each new engagement, his fears for her increased. It was their dream, someday, to leave strife behind, to marry, have a home and children—things impossible even to contemplate for a man who was secretly the Spider!

4

"If you'll excuse me, Nita—Major Dow," he said quietly. "I have a caller who may lead me into more unsolved murders!"

THE MAN, Leary, dismissed first-grade detective of the New York police force, stood stiffly, as if for a uniformed inspection, as Wentworth strode toward him. His jaw had a rigid line that betrayed how he must be bracing himself for this interview. Wentworth held out his hand, and Leary's blue direct eyes widened.

"You—you couldn't remember me, sir!" he stammered. "I—I was dismissed...."

Wentworth clasped his hand. "I remember—and all the details. You left a partner on a stakeout when you heard the criminals you were watching plot to kidnap your fiancée as bait to trap you. You left your post to warn her, and your partner was killed. Commissioner Kirkpatrick had no choice but to dismiss you. However, I know that he thought highly of you."

Leary swallowed stiffly. The eagerness in his face tugged at Wentworth's sympathies.

"I came to ask for a job!" Leary blurted. "I've spent years learning how to fight criminals. I don't know anything else. I'm sure I could be valuable to you, sir!"

Leary was implying no hidden knowledge of Wentworth as the Spider, for, in his own identity, Wentworth had often joined battle with the underworld—had fought side by side with Commissioner Stanley Kirkpatrick, his personal friend. Still, it would be running a chance to take any stranger into his own employ.

Leary held out a broad, strongly muscled hand in appeal. "Mr.

Wentworth," he hurried on, "I think something new is about to break. One of my old stoolies gave me a tip that Knucks Murray is calling his strong-arm gang together at midnight to hear a certain proposition from an outsider. Way I heard it, this outsider is a stranger and he ain't a regular crook. There's something funny about him...."

Thus casually, and without a hint of the horror behind it, Richard Wentworth first heard of the threat that hung over the city, Not even his keen brain could then realize the awful peril, but he knew that, in his experience, amateurs had proved the most cruel and ruthless criminals....

IT LACKED fifteen minutes of twelve when a powerful black limousine glided to a halt on a dark street, within a half block of the apartment building which Knucks Murray owned and in which he made his headquarters. From the car slipped a macabre figure, whose hunched shoulders were sinister beneath a long black cape, whose eyes glittered coldly under the brim of a broad black hat. It was with Wentworth's crisp voice that the figure spoke!

"Bring the coupé to this spot and leave it, Ram Singh," he ordered quietly. "You have your orders."

"*Han, sahib!*" The Sikh's fierce eyes were wistful. "I am to watch the man, Leary. But, *sahib,* you go into danger. May not thy servant...."

His voice died, for the twisted, sinister figure which was the Spider had vanished into the shadows! Moments later, it emerged on the low-lying roofs of the lodging-houses which flanked Murray's apartment and then... the Spider mounted straight up the wall of the apartment building!

From a distance, this performance must have seemed miraculous, but actually the technique was simple. Wentworth had fastened about his waist a belted girdle such as window washers wore, but with much longer

straps. He carried a light telescopic rod. With it, he reached up to the window above and snapped a strap-fastening on the hook provided for the window washer. The Spider went up the strap smoothly, hand over hand, balanced on the sill, and once more used the rod to attach the strap to the next window above. Eight stories to climb. He rose swiftly.

The room Knucks Murray had chosen for his midnight conference had only one door and its windows gave on eight stories of empty space. He lolled on a davenport, a hulking man with a broad, strong-boned face and quick, vicious eyes. About the room, a dozen other men stood or perched on the edges of chairs. Constantly, their eyes strayed to the big man on the davenport. They were killers, yet there was an uneasiness upon them whenever they gazed on Knucks Murray. He lifted a huge fist, yawning, and three men flinched.

The abrupt whir of a buzzer made them all start and, at Murray's gesture, a thin-faced man near the door picked up a telephone, spoke into it. Then he turned toward Murray, a puzzled frown wrinkling his face.

"A guy with a screwy kind of voice says he's on the way up," he said. "Geez, Knucks, he didn't give me no chance to say nothing."

Murray was sitting up straight on the davenport. With no apparent effort, he was suddenly on his feet. His leather-smooth hair, low above his eyes, pulled lower with a scowl.

"So he's just coming up without asking me, is he?" Murray said softly. He laughed, and its sound was high-pitched.

The shoulders of the thin-faced man cringed. "I couldn't help it, Knucks!" he cried anxiously.

Murray waved a big hand. "Skip it."

He stood, facing the door, shoulders hunched, ham-sized fists swinging slowly at his sides. The others watched the door, too. The thin-faced man licked his lips.

KNUCKS MURRAY must have heard or sensed some warning—perhaps a faint click of metal on metal, the slither of a footstep. Knucks' fists stopped swinging at his sides and his chest arched slowly with the bowing of his shoulders. He gave an impression of immense and utterly ruthless power.

It was within two yards of Knucks Murray that flame geysered up from the floor! It started just inside the door and spread upward, a fan of scarlet and white fire. Black tentacles of smoke mushroomed, merged and crept across the ceiling.

Knucks Murray, closest to the flames, did not move. He swayed back an inch, two inches, as a man will before he hurls himself forward—no more than that. His heavily knuckled hands lifted, clenched. Little frightened yelps were lashed out of the other men. Guns leaped into the hands of some—then they froze, motionless, with the hanging jaws of idiots, staring at what stood just inside the door where the flames had gushed.

Not one of them had seen the door open, nor heard it, but a man had entered and stood there with folded arms, harsh, mocking laughter on his lips, as if he had materialized from the flames. *Perhaps* it was a man... The smoky air of the room was sulphurous and reeked of brimstone.

And the figure inside the door was a thing out of legend— out of the hidden, superstitious age of fear when demons had haunted the world of men. From head to foot, he glittered in scarlet. Legs and body seemed to be clothed in scarlet scales that glistened like a snake's. Even his face, with the tuft of beard and pointed mustache, was scarlet.

His eyes shone with the iridescence of flame!

Perhaps Knucks Murray did not wait to see all these things. Perhaps his eyes were still dazzled by flame. But he realized that here was some challenger to his power. His big hands reached out, and he swayed to the attack. The demon figure at the door unfolded its arms with an effect of slowness and cupped a palm beneath its face. Blown from that scale-sheathed palm, a little puff of white dust eddied into the face of Knucks Murray....

If a sledgehammer had crashed into the huge racket leader's face, the effect could not have been more overwhelming. He checked in mid-attack, leaped backward. His giant's hands clawed madly at his face, and he screamed. It was an awful, an incredible sound to come from the throat of a man—formless,

9

tearing… a beast in transcendent agony. The scream was broken by a cough that ripped flesh. Knucks Murray writhed on the floor, and the nails of his powerful hands left bloody welts on his throat. His feet drummed. Where his eyes should have been were little pits of liquid jellies. They *bubbled!*

Through his death agony, a voice rasped. It was deep and grating as if forced from a throat unused to human speech, and the words were like individual blows. The creature of flame and scarlet scales was speaking!

"Your souls are mine! When Hell speaks, you will obey!"

CHAPTER 2
ORDERS FROM HELL

LIKE AN exclamation point to those grating words, the glass of one of the windows smashed inward and through it lunged the hunched and caped figure of the Spider. Twin guns were in his hands, heavy automatics whose slugs could fly with unerring deadliness. They blasted straight at the scarlet horror against the door… and abruptly the creature was not there!

Once more, flame gushed to the ceiling and the black and green filthiness of sulphur-tainted smoke spread a heavy pall. Knucks Murray's last strangling screams were drowned out in the utter panic of his men. Their guns blasted crazily and their cries were without meaning or sense. Only one man kept his head—the Spider!

He realized that, an instant before his guns had roared, the flames had gushed upward from the floor. What had happened in that moment of blinding incandescence, he could only guess. Even Wentworth's keen brain had been stunned by the suddenness of that apparition and the horror of Knucks Murray's death. But superstition had no part in his makeup. It was clever, damnably clever, but he knew that, while the eyes of the men within the room were blinded by the fire, the door had been opened and closed for the entrance of the figure in scarlet scales. He knew that his bullets, hurled at that dread figure, had been an instant too late. The man who spoke with the voice of hell had ducked out once more under the cover of the flames!

Bitter curses tautened Wentworth's lips as he lunged across that room where men had gone mad with terror. In three long leaps, he reached the door and whipped it open. The corridor was empty. There were three other doors, a stairway. With swift strides, Wentworth covered those spots. Fearless, and yet he knew an inward shrinking. He had no defense against that puff of dust that had slain Knucks Murray so terribly....

To the Spider, the death of Knucks Murray was unimportant in that it merely removed from the city one of the racket overlords. The world was better without him. But this thing would not stop here. The mummer who had killed Murray had, in that same moment, taken charge of his huge organization! Eleven of Murray's underlings had witnessed his death and they would obey with trembling any order that came from the man in scarlet. What those orders would be, and what horror this human demon could wreak with his death-powder, Wentworth could imagine only too well! Compared to this creature, Murray had been as innocent and harmless as a child!

Swiftly, Wentworth canvassed the doorways that led from the corridor, found them empty. There remained only the elevator and stairs. Which way had the Master of Hell fled? While Wentworth raced toward the steps, the door of the murder chamber flew wide and men jammed through the opening. Guns were in their hands, their eyes strained wide in drawn, maddened faces. Below, Wentworth could hear a rising fury of shouts and the skating slap of men running along smooth-floored hallways.

The Spider hammered out a blast from his twin guns toward the jammed doorway and, while the panic of his lead gripped the men, he darted up the stairs, burst out upon the roof. The smoky fog laid a nimbus of light over the city; picked up the glow of every neon tube so that it seemed to join in that hell-fire released below. It brightened and dimmed with the flickering of advertising signs. While he wedged the door shut against assault from below, Wentworth scanned the roof by that eerie glow. It was empty....

GUNS WERE exploding in the hallways with a muffled thunder. The panic of the men was venting itself in a killing rage. God help the Spider, if he crossed their gunsights! They would show him small mercy at any time, for they feared not even the law as they did the swift justice of this secret avenger. But tonight... Wentworth's lips moved in a slight, thin smile. Tonight, he, too, had no time to consider such minor matters. Horror threatened the city. Impossible to tell where first it would strike, but there was still something he could do.

With a swift glance, he oriented himself, ran lightly to the balustrade above the window of the room where Knucks Murray lay dead. No chance to use the belts which he still wore twisted about his waist. He swung downward from the overhanging ledge, groped with his feet and found the window. A kick sent the glass crashing inward, a rake of his foot cleared away fragments, then he hooked a heel inside of the casing. Ticklish, death-daring work, with eight stories of space below, even if the tinkle of broken glass brought no one. The Spider scarcely gave it thought. The blasting of guns would cover the sound. As for the rest of it....

Moments later, he dropped inside the room and with long strides reached the body of the gang leader. Even Wentworth's eyes, accustomed as they were to death in myriad awful forms, chilled at Murray's torture-twisted body.

He did not hesitate. From his vest pocket he slipped a slim, platinum cigarette lighter and thumbed open its base. He ground it down upon the forehead of the gangster and, when he straightened again, there gleamed a seal of scarlet, a thing of hairy legs and poison fangs... *the seal of the Spider!*

Madness, thus, to claim as his own the victim of another man? It was all of that. Wentworth could not know what horror the Master of Hell would perpetrate before this very night was out—and because the Spider had claimed one of the dead, the other crimes would be laid at his door! That was a risk he was more than willing to take. He must gain time to find and destroy this demon-man, and it was obvious that the killer wanted control over Murray's mob. If the Spider threw doubt into the minds of the men, left them wondering whether indeed the

RICHARD WENTWORTH.

Spider had slain Murray, they might be slow to obey the orders of their new master. It would give the Spider time....

Nevertheless, a bitter smile was upon Richard Wentworth's lips as he crossed to the window and fastened the first of his straps to the window washer's hook. Tomorrow the newspaper headlines would scream anew for the life of the feared Spider!

THE STREET before the apartment building which was Knucks Murray's headquarters was jamming with police cars. An ambulance howled its hoarse way around the corner, and a white-coated intern dropped wearily from the tail. Policemen on guard beside radio cars sprang to attention as a gray limousine they well knew wheeled to a velvet-soft halt at the curb. A tall, dapper man stepped to the pavement.

"The top floor, Commissioner Kirkpatrick," a sergeant said, hurrying forward. "Knucks Murray was bumped off by the Spider. But the punks have got some screwy idea that it wasn't the Spider at all, but the devil himself."

Kirkpatrick's saturnine face was set in unsmiling lines. "Got the block bottled up tight?"

"A fly couldn't get through, sir." The sergeant saluted.

"See to it that the Spider doesn't," Kirkpatrick said flatly. "I want every man you stop brought before me, and..." He choked

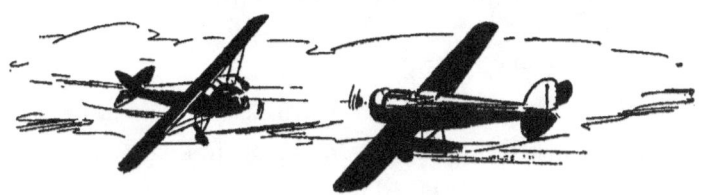

15

off, as a long, black Daimler slid to a halt behind his own limousine and a man in evening clothes, smart with white gloves and high silk hat, moved casually toward him.

"Richard Wentworth!" Kirkpatrick snapped. He went to meet Wentworth with long, choppy strides. "Where did you come from?"

Wentworth lifted his smooth black brows with a hint of mockery. "Why, Commissioner, this is an unexpected pleasure!"

Kirkpatrick stood on widely braced legs, his angular head thrown up challengingly. Under the pointed line of his military mustache, his mouth was straight, uncompromising. These two men were the warmest of friends, but Kirkpatrick was stern in the execution of his duty. Wentworth knew that if ever proof that he was the Spider fell into the hands of the commissioner of police, their friendship would not swerve the course of justice a single point!

Wentworth casually removed his cigarette case, extended it. "I heard," he said quietly, "that Knucks Murray was getting ready for some devilment or another. I was coming down to warn him it really wouldn't do." He looked about him. "I seem to have been a bit late." With this cigarette lighter which could, at his will, imprint the seal of the Spider, Wentworth lighted Kirkpatrick's cigarette. Now in the eyes of both men shone both challenge and admiration.

"You heard. How?" Kirkpatrick waited.

Wentworth shrugged. "A man you dismissed from the force—Leary. He picked it up from a stool pigeon. Leary should be somewhere about." He raised his voice. *"Leary!"*

16

The smile was still on his lips, but it had been a narrow thing—his own escape from the police. Only just in time had he reached his car and sent it hurtling to a safe spot where he could change into his own identity again. Ram Singh's presence meant no disobedience of orders. He had kept watch on Leary… and Leary had watched the apartment building!

From the shadows across the street, Leary's square-shouldered figure moved hesitantly forward, then came marching straight up to where Wentworth and Kirkpatrick stood.

"Leary," Wentworth went on quietly, "entered my employ when the City of New York no longer desired his services."

"Leary," Kirkpatrick said incisively, "I want your answer under oath. How long have you been watching the building? Who has entered and left?"

"On my oath, Commissioner," Leary said quietly, and his blue eyes did not waver from Kirkpatrick's commanding gaze. "Only one man, other than members of the Murray mob, has entered and left that building, to my knowledge."

"Who?" Kirkpatrick's whipcord-lean body swayed forward, waiting for the answer.

Leary frowned. "It's a funny thing," he said. "The man I saw… It looked to me like Modoc O'Malley, the candidate for mayor."

Kirkpatrick uttered an exclamation of disgust. He turned toward the doors of the building. "Wentworth, come with me."

Wentworth lifted his brows again as he deliberately stepped upon his cigarette. "An order, Kirk," he asked mildly, "or an invitation?" He waited for the answer.

Kirkpatrick stopped and faced him. "Either you like, Dick,"

he said softly. "After all, a man of your record is always under suspicion when found near the scene of a crime!"

IT WAS three hours later that Kirkpatrick finally told Wentworth he could go, and for a while the two men stood alone in the room where Knucks Murray lay dead.

"This can't go on, Dick," Kirkpatrick said emphatically. "I know that, somehow or another, the evidence is never quite sufficient to prove you are the Spider. But this—" his eyes flinched from the face of the dead man—"this is ghastly. It is the work of a madman! You are developing into a monomaniac. You and your justice! No one man can sit in judgment upon all his kind and defy the laws of humanity!"

Wentworth drawled, "I'll bear that in mind the next time I run across the Spider. He might be interested in your views."

Kirkpatrick swore violently, staring into the face of the man he revered above all others—and doubted most. "Dick, for my sake—for Nita's sake—give up this madness!"

Wentworth shrugged, though his heart went out to his friend. If only he could work openly with Kirkpatrick! But the forces of the law, handicapped by the safeguards set up to protect the innocent, were working with chained hands against such criminals as he had seen at work this night. As long as madmen arose to imperil humanity, the Spider must travel his lonely, perilous road. Until there were no more criminals—or until the Spider fell upon the field of thankless battle, probably at the hands of some such friend as Kirkpatrick….

Wentworth shrugged. "This is boring me, Kirkpatrick," he said harshly. "I need a bit of sleep, if you don't. If you want to hold me longer, arrest me." He turned sharply toward the door, seeing how the heat of the devil's fire had blistered the paint. He was impatient to go, but not to rest.

Kirkpatrick called his name once more, but it was in appeal, not command. Wentworth closed the door and walked steadily toward the elevators... but there was still that pain in his heart. He loved Stanley Kirkpatrick....

Wentworth had Ram Singh drive past Leary's home and drop him there. "No more until tomorrow," he told the dismissed policeman. "You did yeoman work tonight, even if I did arrive too late. Frankly, I'm afraid I attached too little importance to your information. First thing in the morning, try to get some data on what the Murray mob was planning, then report to me."

Wentworth made sure there were no taxis nearby, then gave Ram Singh an order which sent the Daimler swiftly doubling and redoubling on its trail after leaving Leary—then toward the penthouse home of Modoc O'Malley, candidate for mayor of New York City! Wentworth forced his body to relax against the cushions. Sometimes this constant need for caution irked him. He had no real suspicions of Leary. But the police might be alert. Kirkpatrick's attacks of conscience, his pursuit of the Spider, were spasmodic. Not that his sense of duty ever wavered. It was merely that, too often, Kirkpatrick found himself battling against the same criminals the Spider opposed—when even stern duty dictated that he momentarily allow the Spider leeway to destroy mutual foes....

Presently, Wentworth sat more erectly and, at the touch of a button, curtains screened the tonneau completely. Another button caused the left half of the rear seat to slide forward and revolve. Its back contained a closely hung wardrobe and a makeup tray with which Wentworth could disguise himself. His hands moved deftly about their familiar task. A lotion sallowed his skin, drew it tautly across cheekbones and nose. The nose, itself, altered by putty, became hawk-like and predatory. His lips disappeared, so that his mouth was a gash. False, bushy brows, a lank, black wig… Simple changes, yet the face that peered back at Wentworth now was ruthless and terrible—the face of the Spider!

A black jersey covered his formal shirt, a cape for his shoulders, a broad-brimmed black hat… The Daimler slid to a noiseless halt and Wentworth's touch closed the wardrobe and opened the curtains. The car was parked in a dark side street, and Ram Singh's bearded face peered back at him.

"The man you seek lives on the roof here, *sahib*," the Sikh said softly. "May thy servant attend his master?"

Wentworth smiled into the idolatrous eyes of the brave Sikh. Theirs were two different paths with different goals, and yet they fought side by side. Wentworth served justice; Ram Singh served—the man he worshiped, Richard Wentworth.

He murmured a Hindu proverb which had its parallel in Christian annals, "They also are mighty servants of the one true God—they who only keep the watch."

A BASEMENT entrance, barred by a steel grating, yielded to the Spider's deft manipulation of a lock-pick, and he made his silent way up an interior fire-stair to the roof. From there, he easily reached the terrace of the home of Modoc O'Malley. It was fantastic to believe that this man, who had made a lifelong fetish of public service, could be the Master of Hell who had killed Murray. Yet Wentworth was convinced Leary had not lied.

Kirkpatrick had questioned O'Malley by telephone and received an apparently straightforward story. He had, O'Malley claimed, been unaware that the building was Murray's headquarters. He had gone to a man there who had half-promised to sell certain information which O'Malley wanted to use in his campaign. Yes, it all sounded logical enough—and yet the Spider was convinced that the Master of Hell had made his escape by way of the elevator. As nearly as he could determine, O'Malley had made his exit from the front doors at about the same time the Master had fled.

Wentworth crept along the terrace toward French doors from which yellow light shafted. Flat upon the roof, Wentworth peered through the lowest pane of glass. The room apparently was used as an office. A mass of papers was scattered upon the surface of the desk, and O'Malley was tipped back in a chair, dictating.

A frown contracted Wentworth's forehead as he eased to his feet. It was not the most favorable set-up for his task, but he had need to work rapidly. If O'Malley were innocent, he must be eliminated from the problem. Wentworth had no means of telling whether the confusion he had attempted at Murray's headquarters really would delay the work of the Master of Hell....

Wentworth stepped before the doors, drove his heel against the lock. The glass shattered, and the door swung violently inward. The Spider bounded inside, a gun in each fist. He had a whirling glimpse of the girl staggering to her feet—of O'Malley, arms thrown high as he lost balance and pitched backward in his chair, and then....

The gush of flame sprang upward from the desktop where papers were scattered! Dazzling in its scarlet and white intensity, it blinded Wentworth for the moment. He was aware of roiling black smoke, of a taint of sulphur and brimstone in the air!

CHAPTER 3
KILL THE SPIDER!

THE LAST time that hateful scent had filled the air, Knucks Murray had died terribly, and now Wentworth knew something that was closely akin to fear. He flung an elbow across his face, sprang furiously to one side, and brought up hard against the wall twenty feet from that spurt of flame. If the dust could strike at this distance....

Wentworth's guns quested over the room while his eyes fought the flame dazzle. The fire was gone now, except for a smoldering mass on the desk. Only the thick pall of black smoke rolled greasily across the ceiling, seeped down toward lights and floor. O'Malley shouted harsh, broken curses. The girl was against the opposite wall, mouth strained open in soundless fright. But of the scarlet-clad demon Wentworth had expected, there was no glimpse at all.

Where....

O'Malley rolled to his feet, pale face flushed scarlet. Without pause, he came striding around his desk straight at Wentworth.

"You damned crook!" he howled. "You've destroyed my evidence, but you won't stop me. No one can stop me, I tell you."

Wentworth squeezed the trigger of an automatic, and the lead plucked past within an inch of O'Malley's left ear. He clapped a hand to his head, rocked back on his heels, his mouth gasping.

"Stand there and talk," Wentworth ordered, and his voice held the flat and mocking tones of the Spider. "What kind of evidence was destroyed?"

O'Malley tried twice more before he got out words. His face was as pale as it had been florid. His scanty blond hair stood in stiff spines upon his pink scalp.

"Good God," he gasped, "it's the Spider!"

Wentworth's eyes flicked toward the girl. She had taken a pace forward and was now patting out the fire on the desk with her notebook. At O'Malley's words, her head jerked around. Her brown eyes were stretched very wide, and her lips soundlessly echoed, "*The Spider!*"

Wentworth's thoughts were falling swiftly into line. Either O'Malley, himself, had destroyed the data upon his desk because he had recognized the Spider at once and feared something in those papers would be revealed; or someone else had used the chemical which had started the fire. Wentworth let his gray-blue eyes, hidden in the shadows of his shaggy brows, search the room. There was an open window within less than ten feet of the desk, on the opposite side of the room from the doors through which he himself had burst. Chemical might have been thrown from there....

"Talk fast!" Wentworth snapped. "What evidence am I supposed to have destroyed?"

"The evidence that would have proved that Samuel Marco, with Bolshevik millions, is undermining our native government!"

Wentworth felt relaxation run along his nerves. Campaign ammunition, O'Malley meant. He had a platform which called for clearing out the radicals in the city, Communists and others. Marco was the Communist chairman.

O'Malley was roaring at him in his hoarse speaker's voice. "You're in the pay of Moscow!" he cried. "Marco's millions have bought you in! You killed Murray tonight to keep him from giving me my evidence, and now you have burned the papers. Miss Barnes, call the police. We'll hold the Spider here until they come!"

Wentworth's eyes swiveled toward the girl, saw her reach hesitantly for the telephone. He did not interfere. If, as he was beginning to believe, the Master of Hell, or his minions, had actually been here and destroyed those papers, the police could help to trap him… But it didn't make sense. Samuel Marco, even supposing him to be interested in O'Malley's revelations, would not ally himself with such a fearful underworld killer!

Wentworth caught the girl's voice. "Patricia Barnes, secretary to Modoc O'Malley…."

Patricia Barnes! Why, damn it, she was the fiancée of Donald Leary—the girl whose rescue had cost Leary his appointment as a policeman. Here was fresh mystery. Wentworth moved forward with long strides and seized O'Malley by his coat lapels.

"If you talk fast," he said flatly, "you may save yourself. You honestly believe that I destroyed those papers and that Samuel Marco hired me to do it?"

"Believe?" O'Malley stammered. "Believe? I know!"

At the same instant, he made an awkward attempt to punch Wentworth. The Spider's thrust sent O'Malley spinning to the floor, then he leaped toward the French doors with long, reaching strides. A gun cracked out behind him, and Wentworth felt the stinging burn of a bullet across his left bicep. He dodged behind the casement of the door and had a glimpse of Patricia Barnes, with a small automatic in her fist and a set, grim look upon her face.

Wentworth felt the blood seep warmly down his arm, but he flexed the muscle. Despite some pain, it was not really injured. His eyes were bleak. He had been wrong to discount the girl's courage. A half-second earlier in her timing and that bullet would have drilled his body! Ironic that the Spider should come so close to death at the hands of a mere girl….

THERE WAS a tight frown of concentration on Wentworth's face, as he sprang to a bench set against the wall of the penthouse, leaped, caught the edge of the roof, swung himself up. A glance showed him the roof was empty now, but he scarcely expected anything else. He bounded across to a spot above the open window. Through which, he had guessed, chemicals might have been thrown. The light of a small pocket flash glinted on

25

the metal gutter, showed the scars of a clamp of some sort. By that means, a man could have lowered himself to the window.

Frowning, but with no further delay, Wentworth dashed for the exit of the fire-stairs by which he had climbed to the roof. The police were on the way, summoned by Patricia Barnes. A fleeting smile touched his lips at memory of the girl. She had courage, indeed, opening fire on the Spider! God, he hoped the police would be swift! The man who had thrown the chemical could scarcely have escaped the building yet!

At the entrance to the fire-stairs, Wentworth paused. He threw back his head and a long, ululating wail came from his lips. The cry had a peculiarly penetrating quality and, many stories below, he had no doubt that Ram Singh would hear it, would be on the alert. Between them, they might trap the Master of Hell! Memory of that death-dust came fleetingly to Wentworth's mind, and his throat tightened at thought of Ram Singh meeting his end by such means. But there could be no flinching.

Wentworth took the stairs downward with great leaps. His feet made soft echoes. Along the thick-walled way he traveled, there was no other sound. Straight to the basement he plunged, along the service corridor to the steel grating. He might have overrun the man he hunted, but it would be easier to keep watch from outside. Within minutes, the police would be here to search the interior.

He pushed wide the gate, sprang up the steps to the street and—

"Drop that gun!" a man's voice ordered. "Drop it, or I'll shoot to kill, Spider!"

Wentworth peered toward the voice. His frantic need for hurry had overthrown his usual caution, and he was fairly trapped. The man stood in shadows but light glinted on a leveled gun. That in itself did not matter. The Spider had faced killers' guns before this—but the Spider could not injure innocent men. He had dedicated his life to the service of humanity. Even to save his own life, he would not fire on an honest citizen!

"I'm caught," Wentworth said, his voice strangely harsh and penetrating. "And when a wise man is caught, he surrenders." He uttered a phrase of Punjabi and hoped frantically that Ram Singh was near enough to hear. *Take him, but take him gently, my warrior!* But you probably do not know that proverb, do you my friend?"

"Drop that gun!" the man repeated sharply.

Wentworth let the gun fall to the sidewalk. Damnable to be so close on the trail of that demoniac killer and to be stopped by the one thing which could confound the Spider—an honest man! Dimly, in the distance, he caught the whimper of a police siren. Confound it, he had to get free! He began to inch toward his captor.

"In a few moments," he said quietly, "the police will be here. They will grab all the glory of your capture, if they do not kill me on sight. The police have small reason to love me, you know. As a matter of fact—"

"Take two steps backward!" The man's voice was harsh with tension. "I haven't seen you move, but you're moving. Two steps, damn you, or—"

Wentworth caught a glitter of metal—a thrown knife—flash-

27

ing toward his captor. A cry burst from his lips. He had told Ram Singh to be gentle! The Sikh understood only one thing, that his master was in peril... The man with the gun crumpled without a sound, pitched forward on his face, and the revolver skittered across the pavement. In a long bound, Wentworth reached his side and spun the man over into his arms.

"Leary!" he gasped.

Ram Singh's silent figure stole out of the darkness. "I could not be too gentle, *sahib,* " he said gravely. "I struck him with the hilt of my knife!"

The siren's whimper had become a shriek. Time for the Spider to flee. The police must finish the hunt for the Master of Hell, and there was small chance of success now. The man undoubtedly had got free of the building while Leary held him helpless. Leary... Wentworth peered sharply down at the unconscious man, then slowly shook his head. No, Leary must have come for his fiancée—the girl upstairs. Swiftly, the Spider affixed his seal to the pavement beside Leary. That would clear the ex-detective of suspicion when police found him.

Then the Spider rose and raced away into the night.

FOR TWO vain hours, Wentworth sought to locate the leader of the Communists, Samuel Marco, although O'Malley's accusations against the man still seemed fantastic. In the first place, Wentworth could see no profit for Marco in such machinations as the Master of Hell had started. O'Malley, like all politicians, was eager to seize any pretext to make campaign ammunition. Nevertheless, Wentworth would have been better satisfied if he could have located Marco… The man seemed to have vanished completely.

As time dragged past, the Spider's tension slowly increased. He had imprinted his seal on Murray to gain a little time, hoping that meantime he could find and eliminate the frenetic killer who mockingly wore the garb of Satan. In that he had failed—but another device might be used. If he could hunt down Murray's men, make them believe that it had indeed been himself who had killed Murray, he might be able to impose his orders upon them. Then he could use them to trap this Satan!

Such a course would be perilous in the extreme, but the Spider had never shrunk from danger. He caught up the speaking-tube of the Daimler and gave a low-voiced order to Ram Singh. The eager stiffening of the Sikh's shoulders told that he sniffed battle. Wentworth smiled a little. To the Punjabi, fighting was the breath of life. The Spider's own lot would be simpler, he knew, if he, too, battled for sheer love of it. The sharp challenge of wits could still arouse him—but when the Spider went to war, it was because innocents had died!

So far, only a criminal had fallen beneath the awful death-dust of Satan, but well Wentworth knew that unless he struck surely and at once, that toll would mount terribly. Satan could desire the enslavement of Murray's racket mob for no other purpose than to launch criminal onslaughts against humanity. It was possible that he only wanted control of the rackets—but the tyranny of such a fiend was awful to contemplate!

The powerful Daimler purred to an effortless stop in a shadowed side street, and the Spider slipped to the pavement. He was in a region of warehouses, and in the air was the sharp cool-ness of the before-dawn wind. Far off, an elevated train made an irregular clattering. Ram Singh stood beside him, his arms folded, dark eyes intent upon the face of the master he loved.

"Follow me—at a distance," Wentworth ordered, "but keep within earshot."

As silently as the creature whose name he bore, the Spider stole along the street. Finally, he halted beside a narrow metal door in the brick wall of a warehouse. This was another of Knucks Murray's strongholds—a trucking warehouse from which one of his many rackets operated. There should be some of Murray's men here. Wentworth's plan was simple—to take control of the men and then wait for the message of Satan! When those orders came, he would plan how best to trap Satan himself!

His lean powerful fingers, encased in the skin-like gloves the Spider always wore, manipulated a lock-pick, and he stole into the dark vastness of the warehouse. He could catch no whisper of movement, no murmur of voices, and he crept forward with a tautness of nerves that he could not wholly explain. There should be men and movement here and there was none—that he could detect!

Between stacked crates and barrels, he angled toward the box office, which he knew would be near the main doors of the warehouse. There, if anywhere… Here was a light! Pale threads of yellow squeezed out around an ill-fitted door. Wentworth hastened toward it—then checked, with every muscle set! His nostrils twitched and a prickle ran across his scalp. It was not fear, but... he smelled the acrid odor of brimstone!

With long, soft bounds, he raced toward the door, paused with his hand on the knob. Silence within. He stooped to peer through the keyhole. The dusty interior seemed empty of human life—but now the odor was stronger! With sentient fingers, Wentworth twisted the doorknob. Violently, he thrust the door open and leaped—*backward!*

A low cry sprang to his lips. The office was not wholly empty, for a corpse lay upon the floor—a corpse he recognized even while horror, for the way in which the man had died, made coldness strike at his heart. The man was one of Murray's lieutenants and had been slain by Satan's death-dust!

Still, Wentworth did not rush into the office. Satan had come before him, and now the Spider's plans were wrecked. But there was a square of paper on the dead man's breast—a message, but to whom? Wentworth thought he knew! From a pocket of his cape, he drew out the telescopic rod which he had used in climbing with his window-washer's straps. With it, he reached toward the paper. Not quite long enough. Gingerly, the Spider took a single step into the office, touched the paper....

An involuntary cry sprang from Wentworth's lips. There was a sharp hissing sound that seemed to come from every corner of the office and, instantly, the air was filled with the roiling, swirling white torture-dust of the Master of Hell!

CHAPTER 4
HORROR HORDE

IF WENTWORTH had waited for the sight of the dust to warn him, he would have died there terribly in the trap set by the Master of Hell. Instead, at the first warning hiss, he had wrenched himself violently backward. He tried to slam the door, but his hand slipped from the knob. Frantically, cape thrown protectively across his face, he bolted into the darkness. He struck against a stack of barrels, caromed away and heard them thunder to the floor behind him.

Ram Singh's voice reached him, shouting a question and, from behind the muffling folds of his robe, Wentworth hurled a warning. His blundering flight was desperate, and suddenly a strong hand gripped his arm.

"This way, master!"

Wentworth whipped the cape from before his face.

"Out, Ram Singh!" he urged. "The death-dust may be sucked toward us by the draft. You were a fool, man, to enter here!"

He led the way at a pounding run, jerked out to the street and, once there, he checked. His breath, held so long, came in sobbing draughts, and his eyes burned. This trap meant clearly that Satan not only had been here before him, but had also anticipated his plans. The man was clever—and undoubtedly in complete and undisputed control of Murray's band of criminals!

Kirkpatrick must be warned. If possible, the fiend's plans must be anticipated. Every force must be thrown into the field at once to stop Satan before his power became too great!

Before Wentworth turned homeward through the gray drabness of the dawn, he penciled a note of crude letters and fastened it to the door of the warehouse, signed it with his Spider's seal. This would warn innocent people against the death that lurked within. When, once more, the Daimler rolled through the sonic-operated security gate* of his mansion stronghold behind Sutton Place, the Spider had given place again to Richard Wentworth, though something of the bleakness of that grim nemesis still lingered in his eyes.

The square-jawed Jackson, who had been Wentworth's sergeant in the war, met him with an automatic in his hand, a routine precaution in the Spider's castle.

"Miss Nita is still here," Jackson reported. "At her orders, I admitted Major Dow about one o'clock. He has some information he thinks may be important."

Wentworth nodded. He instructed Jackson to get in touch with a private detective agency he sometimes employed, and obtain detailed reports on Modoc O'Malley, Knucks Murray,

---

* AUTHOR'S NOTE: Because of his frequent battles with the underworld, Wentworth found it necessary to set up a thousand scientific safeguards about his New York residence. The mansion itself, built upon piers, was a small fortress. The two dead-end streets abutting the city block he had purchased between Sutton Place and the East River, were fronted by high, electrically defended walls. The steel gates were operated either by a guard within or by a special sonic device which Wentworth employed. This was a two-toned whistle on which he must blow blasts timed to the split-second in order to open the gates.

Samuel Marco and all their movements during the past week. Softness touched Wentworth's chiseled features, as the elevator shot him swiftly to the third-floor drawing room.

It was like Nita to keep watch… She ran to meet him, her cool hands soft and confiding as they reached for his. Major Dow lifted his stocky frame from the divan.

"I've been trying to lure Nita away from you, Wentworth," Major Dow said equably. "I devote hours to the task. You appear—and she leaves me cold."

Wentworth squeezed Nita's hands. "You were very kind to keep Nita company, Major."

Dow caught up a newspaper, flaunting it, and the black headlines sent tautness through Wentworth's body. He knew their tenor before he read them, blaming the Spider for Murray's death, for the destruction of O'Malley's papers. Through them all ran one theme, *Death to the Spider!*

Wentworth smiled carelessly. "My rival for criminological fame seems to have slipped a little," he said lightly. "My tip took me late to Murray's place, and Kirkpatrick held me. Kirkpatrick is quite indignant… at the Spider."

Dow's face sobered. "That Murray death is a horrible thing as it was described. I'm in Chemical Warfare, you know, and I wanted to tell you—I never heard of anything so horrible, except…."

"Except what?" Wentworth asked sharply.

34

Major Dow shook his head. "It's really an official secret," he said, "but there is a man named Prentice—Captain Prentice—at Aberdeen who was working on something that sounds similar. I'm not acquainted with the details."

Wentworth's face was absorbed, serious. "I wonder, Major Dow, if you can inquire quietly and find whether Prentice perfected his device and whether it is… safe."

"That also is part of what I came to tell you," Dow said slowly. "Publicly, I am on furlough. Actually, I am on detached duty. The war department believes that foreign spies have got hold of Prentice's secret!"

"The spies," Wentworth said softly, "are not always foreign! Major Dow, we'll have to find out from the war department if this chemical used by the criminals could possibly be Prentice's invention. If it is, we'll have to determine whether any means have been found to combat it. There are criminals who, with that weapon, can turn a peaceful country into a shambles compared to which even modern warfare is as harmless as a game of anagrams!"

ONCE THE wheels were set in motion, there was nothing more that could be done at once, and Wentworth flung himself down for a few hours of sleep. It was eight-thirty the same morning, and he was busy with his daily routine of gun practice and saber drill when Donald Leary was announced. Wentworth rested the saber point on his shoe-tip, breathing deeply from the exercise. It was only by such constant work that he could keep body and mind keen for his many battles.

Tenuous coils spiraled above the heads of the police and the death-dealing agony.

Leary had a strip of adhesive just back of his ear, where Ram Singh's knife hilt had struck.

"I think I've got something on the Murray mob, sir," he said

eagerly. "It may not amount to anything, but... Well, I used to guard an armored truck that makes its monthly collections today. Last time I was on it, I spotted one of Murray's men, who seemed to be following us around. I couldn't catch him. This morning I had a phone call, and a man asked me if I'd like to trade some information for money. I should have accepted, but my temper got away from me. Just because I got kicked off the force, crooks think… No matter, sir. It may not mean anything, but that business I picked up yesterday didn't sound like much either—and Knucks Murray is dead!"

Wentworth nodded quietly. His brain conned the information, and his pulses quickened. It sounded suspiciously like the Murray mob were figuring on robbing the armored truck. It might not have any connection with the Master of Hell, but… The Spider would keep watch!

"Patricia Barnes, secretary to Modoc O'Malley," he said curtly, "is your fiancée?"

Leary flushed. "Yes, sir. You read about what happened."

Wentworth nodded, and waited.

"I was going to take her home, sir," Leary said eagerly. "Mr. O'Malley is all right, but she shouldn't work so late."

Wentworth turned away to hide a slight smile. He had been foolish, probably, to suspect young Leary. Wentworth called police headquarters and, on identifying himself, was connected with Kirkpatrick's office. He relayed Leary's information.

"Of course, I'm not interested in Murray's murderer, Kirk," he answered a query. "So far as I can discover, O'Malley has solved the whole thing. It looks like it might be a Communist plot to keep him from being elected mayor."

He turned back to Leary. "That's good work. Keep working your stool pigeons."

Leary was frowning. "But I thought I'd have a chance to help you fight criminals, Mr. Wentworth!" he cried. "I thought I might have a chance to get back on the police force."

"So you may," Wentworth told him quietly. "If I need you, I'll call on you. Just now… *En garde,* Jackson!"

Jackson's saber flashed up, and the steel sang in slash and riposte. For moments, Leary watched, then he turned and went disconsolately away. As soon as he was out of sight, Wentworth cut short the saber drill.

"Don't lose sight of him, Jackson," he said swiftly. "In some way, I'm convinced, he's vitally tied up with the entire business. I believe he's innocent, but… it is strange how he gets information!"

That was all.

Jackson swung the saber in salute and hurried off. It would take some minutes for Leary to leave the mansion and walls.

Jackson could be in the street in thirty seconds by secret ways. Wentworth tossed the saber into the rack, stepped into the showers. After his few hours' sleep, he was alert and ready for battle—but the foe had vanished!

Wentworth was still in the shower when Jenkyns, the aged butler who had served his father before him, entered with a portable telephone. He apologized now.

"The call seemed important, Master Richard."

Wentworth caught up the instrument and slowly, as he listened, his face grew hard and fierce. "Get me the headquarters of the truck drivers' union," he snapped at Jenkyns. He sprang from the shower and began to punish, with a rough towel, his hard-muscled body. Muscles leaped and writhed beneath the satiny skin of perfect condition. There were the white weals of a score of old wounds.

"Police calling," Wentworth spoke raspingly into the phone. "You have the routes customarily used by various trucking companies. How do the trucks of the Mortimer Shippers, Incorporated, start their Jersey runs—Hudson Tunnel? Right."

He was dressed by the time Jenkyns had the offices of the tunnel police on the phone. His swift questions brought out that four trucks of Mortimer Shippers—the concern name under which Murray's warehouse and trucking firm operated—had crossed beneath the Hudson that very morning! It was easy to ascertain, since trucking companies used tickets, bought by the book, rather than cash to pay the toll charges.

Swiftly, Wentworth snatched two heavy automatics from the armory rack on the wall of his dressing room. As he checked their loading and shoved fresh clips into his pockets, he flung swift words at Jenkyns.

"Phone Miss Nita," he snapped, "and give her this message: 'It may not be important, but Knucks Murray and Modoc O'Malley were together in Mill Town, New Jersey, on Tuesday. My private detectives report this. This morning, four of Murray's Mortimer shipping trucks went through the Hudson Tunnel into New Jersey. A few hours before this, the man, Satan, of whom I told her, raided the garage of the Mortimer Shipping Company.

" 'From the morning papers, Miss Nita will learn that the strikers in Mill Town, New Jersey, have been given until noon to cease picketing the Hardesty Factory and return to their jobs. The employers charge that the strike is the work of labor racketeers and Satan is taking over racket mobs!

" 'Miss Nita is to recall what I told her of the way in which Knucks Murray was killed—and to consider what would happen if hundreds of men and women strikers ran into… *a dust storm!*' "

Jenkyns' veined hands trembled as he turned to the telephone. "Master Richard," he said heavily, "Miss Nita will want to know the reason for this message."

Wentworth laughed sharply. He thrust the automatics home into their clip-holsters beneath his arms, punched his fists into a dark topcoat. "It may be necessary for her to take that information to the police!" he said.

"But you, sir!"

Wentworth called back over his shoulder, as he strode toward the door. "I am going to Mill Town!"

CHAPTER 5
DUST STORM DEATH

THE CREW of the armored car was more alert than usual today. It wasn't merely that their collection was heavy—that at the start they picked up over a quarter of a million dollars from a night chain of restaurants. A definite warning had come from the police and, a half block behind them, a radio car prowled. Four men were in the police sedan—one armed with a machine gun and two others carrying shotguns.

Obviously any fool crook would know better than to tackle

the car under these circumstances.

That was what the police thought, too—except for Sergeant Phipps, who had talked for three fast minutes with Commissioner Kirkpatrick.

"We don't know what killed Knucks Murray," Kirkpatrick said, "but we know it was something that burned out his eyes and his throat and his lungs. Something more powerful than any known poison gas. You may go up against that thing today."

Sergeant Phipps' face was white. "But it was the Spider, sir. The Spider don't make war on cops!"

Kirkpatrick knuckled his military mustaches. He said slowly, apprehensively, "A man can go mad."

This was what Sergeant Phipps was thinking about as, beside the driver, he watched the armored car ahead and gripped his machine gun across his knees. He didn't laugh and joke with the other men. Something more powerful than any known poison gas! Something that burned out a man's eyes and lungs....

It was an accident that Wentworth crossed the trail of the armored car. He was driving his coupé rapidly toward the Hudson tunnels, frowning eyes intent on the street ahead. He glanced into the rear-vision mirror and saw the armored car, made out the bony face of Sergeant Phipps in a car behind. They had taken his warning, then! He nodded in approval, palmed his horn at the traffic jammed in the one-way street ahead of him. Loading trucks were parked along one curb....

Abruptly, on Wentworth's left, a truck motor roared, and he kicked his accelerator by reflex, just jumping his coupé clear as a heavy van thrust into the traffic. Wentworth glanced angrily at the driver, and a curse leaped to his lips. He could not be mistaken. That driver was one of the men who had witnessed Knucks Murray's death last night—one of those the Master of Hell had commanded to obey! Even as Wentworth recognized the man, the truck blocked one street ahead of the armored truck!

Wentworth's hand leaped to his gun. Without hesitation, he thrust it through the open window of his coupé and pumped four bullets through the truck's windshield. He did not attempt to hit the driver. He might be mistaken... Even as that thought crossed his mind, he knew that he was *not* mistaken. He was terribly sure that the Master's blow had already fallen. Men were screaming as Knucks Murray had screamed in awful agony, and the cries were muffled as if they fought their way out through steel walls—through the walls of an armored car!

Ahead of Wentworth, the traffic spurted and cleared away as if by magic—melting before the peril of blasting guns. Wentworth leaped from the car. From the cab of the truck, a gun spurted flame at him. Its lead hissed past within an inch of his face and Wentworth's automatic answered like the echo of that shot. This time, he fired deliberately—to kill! The Spider knew how to shoot. The impact of his lead jerked the gunman to his feet, hurled him back across the seat.

In two leaps, Wentworth reached the truck and sprang to the driver's seat. He peered beyond at the armored car. It had rammed its nose against the side of the truck and, from within, a few screams still rose feebly, terribly strangled, tortured. And about the truck swirled and beat the black, sulphurous fumes of the Master of Hell!

The four police, under Sergeant Phipps, leaped from their sedan. They raced toward the armored car with ready guns.

"Back!" Wentworth shouted. "Back for your lives! The death-powder!"

EVEN AS he yelled, something that glittered in the sun tumbled toward the police. Sergeant Phipps glimpsed it, kicked awkwardly to knock the thing aside. His foot connected, and there was a muffled blast like a tear-gas bomb. But it was not tear gas, this white powdery stuff that mushroomed upward! Its tenuous coils spiraled about the heads of the police, and then… agony!

One of the police turned to run, and wisps of the stuff clung and whipped about him as he fled. On his second stride, he began to scream as his comrades, writhing on the pavement, were already screaming. He bent double and pitched to the side-walk. He beat his face against the concrete in his pain.

Wentworth's face was white, eyes blazing with fury. The police were not the only sufferers. A girl hurrying along the walk was caught by a tentacle of the white horror. In her agony, she ran through a plate-glass window. A boy pushing a hand-truck stood rooted to the spot in terror, then turned and tried to flee. He took only three steps… His hand-truck trundled slowly along, rolling after him with the pull of gravity. It stopped when it hit his drumming feet.

It was here, the hell that Wentworth had feared—the white fog… The nearest thing that Wentworth had ever known to physical terror gripped him then, for tentacles of the horror were reaching toward the truck! But, damn it, allies of the killers were here! There must be a protection. Wentworth seized the body of the man he had slain and jumped backward to the street, flung it across his shoulder and ran. Twenty-five feet away, he checked and dropped the man to the pavement.

Across the man's face was a skin-thin mask that fitted every feature of his face. But the mouth and eyes were fitted with rubber-cupped plates. Wentworth ripped it from the dead man, drew it over his own head. He twisted about and, with deft fingers, stuffed fresh cartridges into his automatics. Then with heavy, deliberate tread, he moved back toward the shambles the Master of Hell had wrought.

The screams of the dying had faded, but there were other shrieks now as panic stampeded its wild way along the block. As far away as if it were in another world, a police whistle shrilled and shrilled. Wentworth quickened his pace. He sprang to the truck's running board, levered the seat with his foot and grasped the roof of the cab. He muscled his body upward, lay prone on top the van and peered into the street beyond. Nothing moved there. Faces were thrust from windows. A half-block away, crowds swirled on the street. Wentworth sent a bullet whining over their heads, smashed a show window.

"Back!" he shouted against the muffling filter across his lips. *"Back! Poison gas!"*

The echo of his voice beat against the walls, and the cry was caught up. "Poison gas! Poison gas! *Poison gas!"*

From one of the loopholes of the armored car, a gun roared! Leaden pellets, buckshot, screamed past Wentworth's head, tore up the edge of the roof. He saw then that the back doors of the truck stood open, their steel a perfect guard against his bullets. The looters were already at their work!

At precisely twelve o'clock a rain of death began!

Grimly, Wentworth thrust back from the edge of the roof. His moment would come. They could not flee in the wedged truck.

Something that glittered in the sun lobbed up into sight, arched toward him. A shrinking ran through all Wentworth's body, but he reached up a hand and snatched the bomb in midair. It might be a time-fuse, but the bomb that felled Sergeant Phipps had been the contact type, and....

With furiously swift movements, Wentworth cupped the glass globe in his hat, thrust it at arm's length from him. Then... he screamed. He beat upon the roof of the truck with fists and feet and screamed until his throat ached. He coughed as if his lungs were being torn out.

Afterward, he lay still and, behind the mask, his lips were thin, bitter. A small mirror from his pocket gave him a partial view of the street. He saw two men, half-concealed behind the truck doors, climb to the street with a heavy burden of loot. He leveled his two guns and squeezed both triggers together. One man, shot through the hip, was whirled into the open by the quarter-ton impact of the lead. The leg of the other was smashed out from under him and he slammed to the earth. Wentworth fired twice more, and this time he could choose his targets. The men began to scream....

ONCE MORE a smashing discharge tore at the edge of the roof. Wentworth felt a burning shock along his skull and sagged dizzily, face down, on the roof.

From the truck, the gun roared again and again. An automatic jarred numbingly in his hand, slid slowly across the roof. Near him, there was the muffled blast of a bomb. The cry that surged to Wentworth's lips was not feigned this time. Along his skull, where a leaden pellet had creased, agony ran a white-hot iron!

48

The pain of it jerked Wentworth from his momentary daze. He thrust himself backward, snatched up his hat and jammed it down on his head. The bomb he had snared from the air tumbled and broke at his feet, and the white dust towered about him. The shriek of sirens was rending the air apart. A bullet jerked at Wentworth's coat. Blindly, he leaped from the roof of the truck. The pavement stung his feet, and he fell.

The pain in his scalp was intolerable. He sprang up, reached a car parked at the curb, and the gun flamed in his hand until gasoline spouted from the tank. He thrust his head beneath it. Fortunately, the mask shielded his eyes. The liquid washed clean the wound upon his head. There was a new pain from the acrid bite of gasoline, but that could be borne. Wentworth pushed erect and peered dazedly along the street. He had done a mad thing—leaped to the pavement beside the armored truck. But they must have thought him doomed, for there had been no more gunfire. And the truck was *empty!*

Wentworth peered blearily along the street. The lenses of the mask were fogged, but he dared not remove it for an instant.

The white dust still swirled in the air, danced across a broad shaft of sunlight that slanted down. There were only the dead upon the ground and the two criminals Wentworth had shot.

One of them still squirmed in his agony. But where had the looters fled?

A sudden thought struck Wentworth. There was another question, too. From what point had the death-dust first struck? He dropped abruptly to his knees—and then had the answer. Beneath the truck, a manhole cover was half ajar! The dust had come from there and, that way, too, the killers had fled!

Gun grimly thrust before him, Wentworth crawled toward the manhole. It took minutes to wrestle aside the heavy cover, single-handed. He threw the thin beam of his pocket flashlight into the pit, and his face whitened beneath the mask. As thick as London fog, the white powder swirled down there in the darkness. Even as he stared, he felt it begin to gnaw at the perspiring creases of his hand, between his fingers. Wentworth drew quickly back.

If he had known that, in those underground tunnels, he could overtake the Master of Hell, not even that dread death-dust would have turned him back. But he had not even glimpsed the monster today. There was a greater good he could do—save the inrushing police from the horror that had overtaken their comrades.

Wentworth pushed wearily to his feet. A telephone would warn police headquarters how the looters had fled—warn them, too, against allowing men to invade this area until the death-dust had evaporated. Meantime… Wentworth staggered toward the line of people far up the street, shouting his warning before him.

"Poison gas! *Poison gas!*"

IT LACKED only a few minutes of noon when Wentworth had finished his explanations to Commissioner Kirkpatrick, and the doctor had dressed what looked like a severe acid burn upon Wentworth's scalp. A frenzy was upon Wentworth, but he could not persuade Kirkpatrick to release him.

"You will say it is madness," he said violently. "But I believe the same thing threatens all Mill Town. Confound you, call it a hunch, if you will, but both Murray and Modoc O'Malley have been to Mill Town recently. Today there is a warning there that, unless the strikers break their picket lines at noon, the owner will 'take steps' to end the strike. Furthermore, the man behind all this is seizing control of one racket—and there are charges of racketeering in Mill Town!"

Kirkpatrick smiled slightly. "That is madness, Dick," he said. "No man would dare to unleash such horror as this—to break a strike. As a matter of fact, the owner of the factory was in my office this morning—Gillian Hardesty. He's an old friend of mine. He's desperate, he says, but is also reluctant to hire non-union men to work for him. However, he's finally got his courage up to that point. If the strikers don't give in by noon, that's what he's going to do. That's all. I'm afraid your hunch is wrong."

Wentworth shook himself free of the restraining hand Kirkpatrick put on his arm.

"When have I been wrong in criminal matters, Kirk?" he asked quietly. "Man, I have lived among criminals, spent my life in studying their psychology. I can't give you any logical reasons for my fears, but I tell you *I know!*"

Kirkpatrick's face was worn. He was grief-stricken at the loss of his men. The force was family and wife to Kirkpatrick, and he had given years of his life to the service. His love for the men was a genuine affection and, when they were slaughtered, he was bereaved. That was it.

Slowly, Kirkpatrick turned to a telephone. "I'll have the state police warned," he said. "I'll say it was an anonymous tip!"

Wentworth smiled thinly. "That's a poor substitute. Those strikers are doomed unless they flee to their homes! In God's name, make it strong. I'm leaving for Mill Town myself, at once!"

Kirkpatrick lifted a hand as if to restrain him—let the hand drop without saying a word. The eyes of the two men held.

"Come back soon, Dick," Kirkpatrick said slowly. "I can't believe, after today, that you killed Murray last night. That Spider seal was some trick...."

"Tell that to the Spider!" Wentworth snapped, and strode out of the office. A taxi from the door sped him to his own home, and he raced through the lower floor and into the elevator. Ram Singh sprang in with him.

"Orders, *sahib?*" he asked quietly.

"I'm flying to Mill Town," Wentworth said shortly. "I'll take the amphibian. Make sure the machine guns are fully loaded!"

CHAPTER 6
GATES OF HELL

ALL NIGHT long, beside flaring watch-fires, striking pickets in Mill Town had kept their vigil before the gates of the Hardesty Factory. When the dirty gray dawn crept up the sky, hundreds more trooped to their relief, and their number increased steadily throughout a morning that, beginning brightly, turned drear and overcast before ten o'clock.

It was at that hour they received their warning. Four trucks trundled into the edges of Mill Town. A child stole a ride on the back of the last—then fell screaming in agony to the street. It was tragedy, but those who saw had not heard of Satan's death-dust. Despite maternal grief, the warning went unheeded.

To tell the truth, the strikers had not taken Hardesty's ultimatum too seriously. They recognized in it the last gesture of a defeated man. Let them only put on one more mass demonstration and he must yield! Victory was in their grasp, they believed, and they turned their mass demonstration into a holiday; wives marched with their men amidst jokes and snatches of song. Children played at shrieking games of tag amid the thick-pressed ranks. How could they know that presently those shrieks of glee would... *change!*

At eleven o'clock, Gillian Hardesty's car pushed its slow way to the factory gates and Hardesty, bareheaded, pale-faced, stood to speak. Triumphant shouts drowned him out, and he sat down heavily and went on into the plant. It was the strikers' last chance, and they shouted and cheered for minutes afterward, jubilant as their hour approached.

Perhaps some of them noticed the airplane that swung aloft, far up against the gray sky, or saw the single puff of black smoke that ballooned up from the factory's chimney. It is possible that someone grasped the connection between them. A certain tension began to make itself felt as the minutes raced on toward noon. The crowd was quieter.

A woman tugged at her husband's arm. "Jim, somehow I'm afraid."

Jim threw back his big head, braced his wide shoulders and laughed. "In fifteen minutes now, Hardesty makes his play. Fifteen minutes after that… we will win!" He was a stalwart man full of vigor and confidence… *now.* Later… A young wife bore her young son in her arms, and he fretted a little. Perhaps the baby was hungry or the strange, psychic warnings of childhood troubled him—as dogs will whimper on the eve of disaster or rats leave a ship that is doomed. His mother thought that he was hungry. She walked over and sat upon the running board of a parked car and gave him her breast.

"I'll be with you, soon, Frank!" she called back to her husband. *Soon, yes—it was seven minutes of twelve!*

A boy who was playing tag with his companions stopped in the middle of a chase and turned to look for his mother and father amid the marching strikers.

"Aw, let's quit," he yelled at the other children. "It's almost time, and besides… I'm tired."

They jeered at him, but he turned his back on the others and went looking for his mother and father. He would never find them….

There were two airplanes overhead now, and the drum of their motors forced its way into the attention of the thousands packed before the factory. They swung in slow circles, spiraled upward into the clouds. A few spattering drops of rain began to fall. It was one minute of twelve.

The boy tipped back his head to watch the planes climb into the clouds and a drop of rain struck upon his cheek. It made a faint, wet tracery and, as it glided downward the flesh turned pink, turned red. A threadlike fume arose from the spot, and a startled scream burst from the boy's lips—startled, then agonized. The flesh turned black. He danced and ground at his cheek with his hand, and the agony spread.

He was the first. As if the heavens had awaited the signal of that scream, the rain began to fall more thickly, the drops heavy, dense and *fuming!* It was precisely twelve o'clock....

IT LACKED seven minutes of twelve o'clock when Wentworth ripped his amphibian free of the waters of the East River and, with motor roaring wide open, slanted off to the south at a perilously low altitude. Baffling wind currents thrust up at him from the canyons on the streets.

He passed the Empire State Building on the level of its sixtieth floor, and the windows were white with startled faces. Once his insufficiently warmed motor faltered, and the plane sagged. He dived, jockeyed the throttle and raced off once more, skimming the rooftops. He was over Jersey City before he gained a thousand feet of altitude.

When his plane's chronometer registered twelve o'clock, he was still four miles from Mill Town, hurtling along below the cloud level. He had a hazy view of the multitude about the factory gates, but of the boy screaming and prancing in his agony, he could see nothing. He saw a convulsion rip through the crowd—saw its fringes become tattered as individuals, then groups of a half-dozen or more, took flight. That was just before the thickening of the rain drew a gray veil across the horror below.

He could not see the young wife on the running board of the car with a baby at her breast, nor hear her scream as raindrops slashed agony across her face and tender flesh. She bowed her body protectively above the child. While her body jerked and quivered with the lash of fire, she battled her way into the car. She thought that the roof would protect her.

"Frank!" she screamed to her husband. "Frank, oh, please come!"

Frank heard that piercing cry even through the daze of his own pain and tried to answer, tried to run toward her. His back was a sheet of burning agony and the fumes of his own seared flesh strangled him. But scores of others were also rushing toward the cars for protection. A man ripped open the door where the wife and her baby crouched. Before he could enter, a half-dozen others slammed into him, drove him face down to the floor.

The wife had just time to turn her back, to make a sheltering arch of her body above the baby. Panting, fighting human animals, convulsed with pain, crowded in against her. She tried once more to call for Frank, but there was no breath left for that. Twenty people were jammed in a space meant for five, and still others tried to force their way in. Then that incredible rain began to eat its way through the cloth top of the car. A dammed-up torrent of it poured down upon the nape of the girl's neck, just where the black hair made little ringlets against the soft white flesh....

High above, Wentworth was peering down desperately to find the thing that was scattering the crowd. There was no roiling dust, no trace of the four trucks he was hunting. Yet, even above the drum of his motor, the vast inchoate, agonized voice of those suffering humans came faintly to his ears. A spattering of rain rattled over his windshield, across the wings. Abruptly, his head whipped about. Where those drops had touched, the fabric of his wings was dissolving in dark, fuming blotches!

A shout of anger tore from Wentworth's lips. In an instant, he grasped the horror of the thing below even while hand and feet wheeled the ship upward and back out of that destroying fury—the rain. Savagely, he vaulted the amphibian up into the clouds. No question now of how Satan was striking. Somewhere, in this floating fog-bank of death, there must be planes which were spraying out the white death-dust. Somewhere... but where?

Fog, pushing gray and thick against his windshield, gave him a visibility of no more than a hundred feet. Shreds of it tore across his wings as he bored higher. His lips were grim, as he flung a glance now and then at the broad supporting pinions of his plane. The brownness was running along their leading edges. He was still amid the burning stuff. Then the plane that spread it must be higher!

How long would his ship resist a rain that burned like drops of fire? How long before the fabric would rip from it and plunge him down to his death? For the moment his cabin protected him, but if he were forced to take to his parachute, he would not survive a full minute! He peered upward at the overhead glass and saw that, along its edges, the fuming drops were at work. He dodged aside as a spattering of liquid ate through and sprinkled down into the cabin. Where they struck, dark spurts of vapor arose and their acrid stench clogged his nostrils.

Wentworth's eyes flew to his instruments. He dared not climb at any steeper angle. His motor labored at full throttle. Even as he looked, the ship faltered and he was forced to thrust the stick forward fractionally to prevent a stall.

Even as the thought glanced across his brain, the clouds thinned above, and a moment later he burst through into the incredible clean sunlight of the upper spaces. The heat of the sun reached through into the stench-laden cockpit. The wind of his speed swept the wings and fuselage clean of fumes, but a scattered drop spread splatters across the back of his hand on the stick, and he winced at the pain of it.

Swiftly his eyes conned about him, and a shout burst from his lips! There, within less than three hundred yards of him, a plane circled slowly and, from vents beneath the fuselage, poured out a white dust that could only be the death-powder of Satan. A quarter of a mile away, another plane spilled its horror upon the world beneath!

WENTWORTH'S AMPHIBIAN spun about. His thumbs hovered over the trigger-trips of his machine guns. But, quick as he was, the nearer ship, more maneuverable than the heavier amphibian, dodged aside. With the same movement, it swept upward and roared toward Wentworth with the death vapor still spurting from its understructure! Wentworth did not need to wonder at his fate should that white powder trail across him—but there was no faltering in the strong lean hands upon the controls.

Imperturbably, he pulled up the nose of the amphibian to the stalling point and his thumbs were heavy on the trigger-trips. He saw the greasy smoke of his tracers stab into the tail of the murder-ship, then he pulled the stick back into his lap.

It was a mad, suicidal thing to do. The amphibian, already stalling, stood on its tail for an instant. The controls went mushy and useless. Then the ship slid screaming down through space in a whip-stall that wracked its weakened wings and shook all the frail fabric in a frenzy close to destruction. But on Wentworth's lips, there was a faint, bitter smile!

He had seen his tracers strike home through the cockpit of the other enemy ship!

Wentworth, for seconds, made no attempt to correct the fall of his ship, other than to hold the controls rigidly in neutral and allow the motor to race on a full throttle. He was, he knew, diving through a concentration of the consuming rain cloud. Once more the gray fog swirled blindingly against his windshield. And somewhere near, he knew, that other plane was streaking downward with a dead man at the stick! If it should loom in his path, or catapult on him from above, he was doomed.

Out into the gray darkness below the clouds flashed Wentworth's plane and, as he eased back on the stick to zoom once more to the attack, he had a wheeling glimpse below. What he saw turned his face white with despair. The very earth was turning brown under the assault of the rain. He spotted the wreckage of a half-dozen cars that had tried to flee from the slaughter, and the crowd about the fences of the factory....

The leader of the strikers, Big Jim, had gathered his wife into his arms to protect her. He jerked under the pelting of the fiery bullets from the sky, but his hoarse voice lifted in coherent command.

"Through the gates, men!" he shouted. "Hardesty is doing this. Under the roof of the factory we'll be safe."

Wentworth could not see him, nor yet hear his words, but he saw the concerted rush of the strikers for the factory gates. Those steel barriers yielded in an instant to the pressure of thousands, and the mob poured across the brown lawn that had been a neat greensward. He saw the clothing melting away from their bodies, men fall writhing to the ground, clawing the earth, lifting frantic hands to a heaven that was worse than merciless....

So much Wentworth glimpsed and guessed before his amphibian zoomed up once more through the smoking gray horror of the cloudbank. He dared not look at his wings now. He could feel the shuddering, as the wind plucked at torn fabric. There was a wrench. The right wing sagged and he whipped over the stick to compensate. That meant a big strip of the covering had torn from the wing....

Then, once more, he vaulted out into the fantastic brilliance of the sunlight that contrasted so terribly with the fire-drenched earth beneath.

Only one ship still circled the upper heavens. As Wentworth's battered amphibian forced its crippled way upward, this other plane wheeled to the attack. A quarter mile away, it raced toward him with the assurance of an eagle pouncing upon a dove. Wentworth's jaw thrust leanly forward and his hands were steady as he soared to meet the foe. He put his nose straight at the other ship, pulled back the stick. He opened the throttle as much as he dared, and held it there.

Crimson spurts of flame began to flicker from the cowling of the other ship, as its machine guns opened up. Wentworth did not fire. He knew his guns and ship perfectly; he was too far away for effective shooting. His motor made a shield. Bullets might cripple that, but it would be impossible for them to penetrate. He was more wary of the death-powder dusting from the tail of the enemy.

The space between them narrowed incredibly fast. Wentworth saw at once that he could not hope to gain the altitude over the other ship. The other pilot recognized that, too, and, sheering off from the attack, began to climb in a steep spiral. Stubbornly, Wentworth held his course, watched the death plane rise. The dust made a murk across the sun, but it was hundreds of feet above him. He had time—only a few seconds, but time.

Cautiously, he reached out a hand and fumbled with the fastenings of the door. Impossible to push it open against the slipstream at high speed. But if he pulled the pins from the hinges, the slipstream itself would rip the door free. Wentworth was drilling into the wind. Already, he estimated that he was beyond the place where originally the death-powder had been spread. He leveled off, and his speed mounted. Above him, the other plane wheeled—and dived to the attack!

Wentworth watched narrowly. He kicked his rudder to dodge

bullets, but made no other effort to avoid the enemy—until the murder-ship was less than a quarter of a mile away. Then Wentworth did a fantastic thing. He spun in a tight virage, flying straight at the other ship! For a space of seconds, he held that course while his machine guns stammered. The other pilot had terrific speed with which to dodge. He dived—and Wentworth dived, too! At the same instant, he wrenched the last pin from the door hinge and hurled himself bodily against it!

The door was plucked free and, even as Wentworth hurtled into space, he felt the jar when the door ripped through elevator and stabilizer. The slipstream seized and tumbled him crazily. Something brushed his arm, and it went numb. He had a wheeling glimpse of sky and cloudbank, of two planes suicidally close together. He tried to steady himself, to hold that view, but his body tumbled and he lost sight.

Then a shout of triumph ripped from his lips. He half-felt, half-heard a terrific concussion—the tearing fury of two planes meeting in midair! There was a flash of flame that stabbed ruddily down into the fog when he fell, then silence save for the shriek of wind-plucked wires on the falling planes, as that wild harper, death, played upon them.

CHAPTER 7
SATAN'S OWN

WENTWORTH'S HAND was locked on the ripcord of his parachute. His left arm swung numbly at his side, struck by some part of the plane as he had leaped.

He allowed himself to plunge down, down. Had he fought his way far enough upwind to escape the death-dust mingling with the rain?

But there was another reason why he dared not yet pull open the 'chute pack. There was a strong wind. Drifting with it, he would be almost certain to be carried into the area of death-dust. No, he must wait… Slowly, the tension went out of him. He was in a world of tumbling gray fog, but he felt no sting of the burning liquid upon his cheeks.

An instant later, he shot out of the clouds and had a wheeling glimpse of green-covered earth and autumn-stained trees beneath him. It was dangerously close. He jerked out the pilot 'chute, felt the wrench of tightening shrouds and, almost immediately, was flexing his legs for a landing.

He tumbled to earth, and the whooping wind snatched his parachute and dragged him until he could spill the air from it by dragging in the shrouds on one side. He staggered to his feet, heard a far-off crash and saw the towering black smoke as the smashed planes hit the earth. Already, he was working frenziedly on his straps.

The two planes were destroyed and no longer could deluge Mill Town with their fearful death, but Heaven alone knew whether medical aid had yet been summoned to the hundreds of afflicted there. Wentworth abandoned the 'chute and set off at a loping run across the fields. He had spotted a farmhouse over there….

Fifteen minutes brought him to the farm. But it was another twenty before, driving an ancient truck he had been compelled to buy, he reached a telephone. The call went swiftly now to the state police.

"Disaster call for Mill Town," Wentworth snapped. "Hundreds are dying and injured. Acid burns. Confound it, man, there is no time to argue! Get the call to your radio patrols, if you wish, and verify, but remember I shall hold you strictly to account! The newspapers shall hear of any delay. Certainly, I'll give my name. It's Richard Wentworth, of New York!"

The man's tone modified instantly. Wherever police work was done, that name was known—not always favorably, from the strict view of law enforcement, but the police knew well that he would not fabricate such a thing as this. When the call had been sent, Wentworth threw further information at him.

"The chemicals were brought from New York City in trucks of the Mortimer Shipping Company," he hurried on, "and passed through Hudson tunnels shortly after eight o'clock. The chemicals were spread over Mill Town from two airplanes. Those planes have been destroyed now, but I have their numbers and it may be possible to check airports for them."

Wentworth swore under his breath as he strode out to the antique truck he was driving, but there was no car available at the filling station from which he had phoned. He flung himself to the seat and sent the truck trundling down the highway toward Mill Town, twenty miles away. He wracked the machine. Its motor wheezed and steamed. He was doing all of forty miles an hour.

The road he traveled was strangely deserted, and presently he knew the reason. On either side, the grass ran brown to the roadside; trees were desolate skeletons. A cow lay dead in a meadow, its body scarcely identifiable; before a house lay the pitiful, still corpse of a woman. And it was still five miles to Mill Town!

THE HORROR of that ride left Wentworth gaunt-eyed and shaken when he reached the factory site itself. He was forced to abandon the truck and go on foot for the last half mile because of… what lay in the streets. The rain had ceased and in the west the sky was clearing. There was even a hint that the sun might break through.

The blood was drained from Wentworth's very lips; his heart was barren even of curses. There was a reek of death and the poisonous stench of the fire-rain. He was almost beside the factory building itself, and the bodies lay more thickly upon the earth. The steel gates were broken from their hinges. The door of the building itself was smashed inward. Wentworth started toward it… and stopped. The thin wail of a living creature came to his ears. Good God—a baby, alive, amid all this!

Wentworth ran swiftly toward the sound, blanched as he shrank back from the shambles inside what had been a car. The charred body of a woman was hunched over the infant. He knew it was a woman because the remnants of a skirt still clung about her legs.

Across the baby's temple was a single burn, but it was otherwise unharmed. Wentworth took it in his arms before he strode on toward the factory building. That broken door had prepared him, in part, for what he would find, but no man could have conceived such utter desolation. Gillian Hardesty was, of course, dead. A wide-shouldered man, literally eaten up by the death-

rain, had crushed Hardesty's larynx with clenched hands. Wentworth could not know, but this was Big Jim.

Wentworth looked beyond and frowned. The office safe had been ripped open and its contents stolen! On the moment, Wentworth's head snapped up and he went pounding toward the door. The baby, nestling contentedly in his arms, raised a small cry of protest, and tenderness touched the harsh curve of Wentworth's lips. He slowed his pace and, emerging from the factory, threw a sharp glance about.

THE EMPEROR FROM HELL

Wentworth's head smashed into Satan's face and
together they catapulted back against the wall!

That looting could mean only one thing. Satan had played a double-barreled deal here. Undoubtedly, he had been engaged to break the strike, though Hardesty must have been unaware of the means that would be employed. Labor racketeers! Wentworth could conceive of no human who would deliberately engage in such wholesale slaughter... His eyes turned bleak. Yet the creature who assumed Satan's identity had done it!

Hardesty had paid—and Satan had looted in the wake of his death-rain. Remembering how widespread the destruction had been, Wentworth's mind flashed to the neighboring city of Maraucus. Maraucus was no more than three miles from Mill Town. If it, too, had been deluged... God, there could be no question of it! Satan would not have missed that chance. His looters must have been there, too—or might even now be at work!

Desperation surged through Wentworth. He began again to run, soothing the baby as best he could—regained his shambling truck and turned it back to the main highway. The minutes that dragged past were endless, but finally he saw a car burning the road toward him. Deliberately, he drove his truck broadside across the highway and stepped to the pavement with the infant in his arms.

The speeding sedan slued to a halt, and a girl sprang from it. With a jerk of utter surprise, Wentworth recognized her as Patricia Barnes, secretary to the ubiquitous O'Malley and fiancée of Donald Leary!

"No need for you to go on," Wentworth said, and the flatness of his voice shocked even his own ears. "Mill Town is wiped out—except for this infant."

The girl uttered a low, broken cry. "Wiped out!" she gasped. "Oh, Mr. O'Malley was afraid of something happening! He sent me here to investigate Samuel Marco's activities when he discovered Marco was coming to Mill Town today. But… wiped out! You… Oh, I know you—you are Richard Wentworth!"

Wentworth said shortly, "There is no time to lose. Get me back to Maraucus at once. Or better, take the child and let me drive. There is looting going on."

There was a doubt in Patricia Barnes' eyes that seemed strange to Wentworth. He sensed that it had nothing to do with what he had told her, or with O'Malley's suspicions of the Communist leader, Marco. She took the baby with tenderness and bowed her head over it as she turned back to her car.

It seemed to Wentworth that she moved awkwardly. Just as he passed her, she stumbled, reached out a quick, grasping hand to his arm. Her fingers closed with surprising strength directly on the spot where her bullet had raked him the night before! It was only by a violent effort that Wentworth repressed wincing at the pain. But suddenly he knew why her eyes had shown doubt. For some reason, she suspected that he was the Spider! The sight of him, with a rescued infant in his arms, had seemed a strange thing… Wasn't the Spider a murderer?

THERE WAS a faint, twisted smile on Wentworth's lips as he whirled the car and sent it racing toward Maraucus. Altruism was so rare a thing in the world that the people for whose happiness Wentworth gave his life were totally unable to understand his motives. He killed, therefore he must be brutal. There was no bitterness in Wentworth's heart at the thought—only pity. Patricia Barnes' suspicions of him he ignored, for the present. There were more pressing matters at hand!

His quick question to the girl elicited that she had not driven through Maraucus, but had remained on the main highway until the Mill Town turn-off. So she could tell him nothing of how the nearby city had fared. But the roadside desolation told him—too well. They passed two cars, wrecked beside the highway, but the havoc that had been done to their metal left no doubt as to the fate of those who had been within them. Patricia Barnes drew in a shuddering breath.

"Is it—like that... in Mill Town?"

Wentworth's silence gave her a better answer than any words. With a pitying cry, she bent again over the baby whose tiny hands tugged at her breast.

The outskirts of Maraucus were flashing past. Electric and communication wires lay in tangles on the pavements. A corpse sprawled in the middle of the street. Wentworth swerved around it, raced on. Now, suddenly to his ears, was borne the crepitation of distant gunfire! A savage burst of laughter drove out between his set lips. The looters were still at hand, then! *Vengeance!*

With a strong effort, he calmed himself, aware of Patricia Barnes' startled eyes. Vengeance, yes, but another purpose drove the Spider now. If he could capture only one of Satan's men alive, he thought that he would find the means to make him talk! For him, there need be no mercy—ally of a fiend!

Frightened faces peered from a few doors, but death had

stalked too terribly here for anyone yet to dare the streets. The gunfire was closer. Wentworth braked violently.

"I'll leave you here," he said swiftly. "It will be dangerous where I am going."

Patricia Barnes stepped to the pavement. "I think you are a good man, Richard Wentworth," she said softly.

Those words rode with Wentworth as he hurled the car on. It was good to hear a woman's soft voice speak so—to know someone who suspected him of being the Spider might still find in her heart some reverence for him and his work. God knew such moments were rare enough… He whirled a corner, and a shout broke from him. Ahead was a truck whose tailgate bore in huge letters the name, *Mortimer.* Also, jammed across the street to block its progress was a car he recognized—his own Daimler!

That was all he glimpsed before he jerked the sedan to a halt and leaped out. Gunmen were crouched in the cab of the truck and on the ground beside it, returning savagely the fire of two weapons that spoke from the Daimler.

One of the criminals spun about to confront Wentworth, but the Spider's automatics leaped to his hands and blasted in the same instant. Lead picked up the man and hurled him sprawling across the mudguard of the truck. Crouched beside Patricia Barnes' sedan, Wentworth continued to shoot with the deadly coldness that made him so formidable. His aim was unerring, and the two automatics slammed with the steady evenness of a machine.

Two other men were exposed. One took a bullet through the skull as he twisted about. The force of it lifted off his scalp and drove his huddled body a full yard along the pavement where he lay. The second man Wentworth deliberately shot through the gun arm. He went down, screaming, and Wentworth darted forward.

Guns still spoke from the cab of the truck. He had accomplished within moments all that he wanted. He had wreaked vengeance and he had a captive whom he could question—the one he had wounded in the arm. Those men in the cab... Close against the side of the truck, Wentworth thrust a gun through the open window of the cab and pumped out the rest of the bullets. The muzzle of his convulsing automatic swiveled like a machine gun. Afterward, there was silence. The guns in the Daimler were quiet, too, and for a moment desperate fear settled over Wentworth.

HE TWISTED about, heard a woman cry out and then a single spiteful pistol report. The man he had wounded jerked once and then his legs quivered and jerked in dying spasms, a bullet through his skull. It was plain the man had got hold of his gun again and tried to shoot Wentworth down from behind. Wentworth's life was saved, but he swore bitterly at losing this possible informant.

Wentworth's own carelessness had done it, but he had been cheated of a man from whom he might force the truth about Satan. Without hope, he yanked open the door of the cabin. For an instant, he stared inside, then slammed the door again. A .45 caliber bullet does fearful execution at any distance, but at a range of less than a yard....

Wentworth walked heavily toward the Daimler, then his step quickened, and he cried out eagerly.

"Nita! Nita, my dear!"

An instant later, she was close in his arms.

"Oh, Dick," she gasped. "I almost didn't shoot in time! I didn't know that man was there on the ground alive. I was coming toward you, and I saw him move…Thank heavens you've taught me how to shoot!"

The curve of Wentworth's lips was tender. "I thank heavens, too," he said. "But why in the world are you here?" Swift alarm shook him. "What has happened?"

His glance shot beyond her, saw Ram Singh stolidly reloading an automatic beside the Daimler. His turbaned head was proudly lifted. This was the battle that Ram Singh gloried in, fighting for its own sake. Wentworth's eyes probed the violet gaze of Nita.

"Yes, much has happened," Nita told him rapidly. "I had to get in touch with you at once—and there was no way except to come here. Major Dow phoned that this Captain Prentice he mentioned, as inventor of a war chemical, has been found dead in the same way that Knucks Murray was killed. That makes it certain that this man you call Satan has got hold of a government secret."

She went on. "Major Dow still believes that foreign spies are responsible, and O'Malley has filled the papers with charges that the Spider is allied with Communist powers."

Wentworth laughed shortly. "Do they know the nature of Prentice's invention? My own belief is that this dust powder is the anhydride* of some incredibly powerful acid—worse than anything known to science before. When the dust was sprinkled from planes into rain clouds, it combined with the rain to… Well, Mill Town is wiped out."

He continued. "Also when a bit of it got in a scalp wound I suffered—nothing serious, Nita, dear—it immediately burned the devil out of me. When I washed it off with gasoline, there was no further trouble. But if I had used water, I might not be alive to talk of it now!"

Nita's hand lifted caressingly to his forehead. "I knew of that wound," she said. "Jackson reported a curious thing. He said you set him to follow Leary and he saw the man pick up your hat from the street where the armored truck was held up. Jackson did not interfere because he thought Leary meant merely to return it to you. Now he thinks he did wrong. Leary went to his home and afterward mailed a package somewhere. Jackson thinks it was your hat!"

Wentworth frowned at the news but could make nothing of it—until he remembered that Patricia Barnes had grabbed his arm directly on the wound she had inflicted while he wore the garb of the Spider. He smiled now, a little wearily.

"Anything else, dear?" he asked quietly.

Nita nodded. "Tragedy," she said. "The death-dust was used throughout an apartment house off Central Park West. Every

---

* AUTHOR'S NOTE: An anhydride, in chemical terms, is a substance which combines with the elements of water to form an acid. There are other meanings for the word, but this is the sense in which Wentworth uses it here.

person in it was killed, including a number of racketeers. Ghost Lawson was one of them."

Wentworth swore softly. "That means Satan is taking over Lawson's mob also! This is damnable! Unless we stop the man soon, he will be emperor of all the rackets! From there to utter anarchy and criminal rule is only a step!"

Abruptly, Nita screamed and tugged violently at Wentworth's arm. Off balance, he pitched forward and together they fell to the street. The hammer of the machine gun was incredibly loud, the snarl of bullets only inches from Wentworth's head. As he fell, he thrust Nita violently from him, whipped out an automatic.

He hit the pavement rolling, and his gun blasted almost immediately. A gunman who crouched half behind the tail of the big truck was blown violently backward. His head hit the pavement sickeningly—and beside Wentworth something exploded with a soft, muffled explosion that brought a cold stab of fear to Wentworth's vitals. That could mean only the white death-powder of Satan.

"Roll, Nita!" he cried. "Roll and run! Don't breathe!"

He risked that quick gasp to help the woman be loved, though he knew that even that breath might suck the deadly stuff into his own nostrils. He could not roll away himself, blocked as he was by the wheels of the truck. He scrambled to his knees and vapor rolled toward him… not white, but *blood red!*

It was so incredible that for the moment Wentworth believed that his eyes were playing him false. He was on his feet, even as he spotted that eerie death-cloud. Already, the tendrils of the vapor were enfolding Nita where she scrambled toward the curb. Wentworth tried to run, and his nostrils seemed to close and shut off his breathing. His eyes burned. Nevertheless, the impetus of his leap carried him forward, toward the dead machine-gunner his bullet had spilled in the street. He could see the man, hazily. His own feet were without feeling and missed their firm grip on the street. He stumbled and knew that he was falling. But he did not feel himself strike the earth….

CHAPTER 8
A TRAP IS BUILT

IT WAS a half hour later that Patricia Barnes found her car abandoned on Main Street in Maraucus. She still carried the baby in her arms. It had fallen asleep, its weight warm against her breast. She was smiling a little, in the soft way a girl will… until she saw her car.

The sedan was almost in the middle of Main Street, and in the windshield were three jagged holes grouped close together. There were tears in the roof where the bullets had gone out. No blood was on the seat, but on the pavement ahead, she saw dark ugly stains. Nothing else was on the street—no bodies, no other cars. Only there was a faint, sweet odor in the air that made her feel a little dizzy. She got into the car and started it rolling. She went up over the curb in one place to avoid one of those dark stains. On the seat beside her, the baby still slept.

She was ten miles out of the city when she was stopped by state police. When she had identified herself, one of the police took the baby to a nearby hospital and let Patricia drive on. The baby cried after her at the end. From time to time small shudders trembled over Patricia's body. She felt sick, feverish. So much horror....

Sunset-glow lay red across the high buildings when finally she halted her sedan before the New York apartment house where she lived with her mother, and a half hour later, Donald Leary plunged excitedly up the stairs.

"I've got him, Patricia!" he shouted from the door. "I've got the Spider!"

Patricia ran from the kitchen, and her face felt drawn and stiff. Donald was shaking two sheets of paper at her.

"Look!" he cried. "The blood matches, every way! Count! Coagulation! Type! The smear you got when you wounded the Spider, and the blood on Wentworth's hat! It's not final evidence, but it will help like hell! I've got the rest of it all worked out!"

Patricia Barnes dropped down on the overstuffed davenport. From the bedroom her mother's voice came out querulously. "You haven't been to speak to me yet, Donald!"

Donald glanced impatiently toward the door, then went in dutifully. Patricia Barnes' hands trembled as she looked blindly down at the two sheets of paper. When Donald came back, she stood up and put her hands on his shoulders. She looked up into his face very seriously.

"Donald," she said, "you can't do it! I... I'm sure Mr. Wentworth is the Spider. I caught hold of his arm where I wounded the Spider, and he tried to keep from showing pain. But I did feel the muscles twitch, and I felt the bandage...."

"Where was all this?" Donald Leary interrupted excitedly. His eyes were staring, shining. The muscles worked along the line of his broad jaws as Patricia told him of the things that had happened in Mill Town and Maraucus.

"If you could have seen how tenderly he held that baby!" Patricia cried. "He—he's a *nice* man, Donald!"

Leary laughed. "Sure, he's a nice man! Do you know how many men the Spider has killed—with his own hands, I mean? I checked it up on the police files today. More than two hundred

DONALD LEARY

PATRICIA BARNES

SAMUEL MARCO

RANDOLPH DOW

MODOC O'MALLEY

men with the Spider seal actually on them! How many more there have been, God only knows!"

"They were criminals, Donald! Every one of them, I'm sure!"

Donald Leary drew Patricia to the davenport beside him. "Darling," he said, "cops can't consider whether a man is justified in killing another man. All we know is that it's against the law to kill. If the courts want to set him free, that's not our business."

"You're not a cop anymore, Donald," Patricia said quietly.

Leary's face flushed. "I can be! If I can prove Wentworth is the Spider, why... they'd damned near make me commissioner! They'd have to! Look, Patsy, I've got the whole thing worked out. I just keep on the Spider's trail and, sooner or later, I find a man dead with the Spider's seal on him. I get a ballistic record of the bullet, and then all I've got to do is take the gun that matches it off Wentworth when there are witnesses! With the blood, and the evidence you can give, we'll sew him up tight!"

Patricia came sharply to her feet. "I won't do it, Donald!" she cried. "I think it's a dirty trick, getting a job with him and then trying to trap him!"

"Pat! We planned that all out together!"

"But... But I hadn't met him then!" Patricia flung her arms about Leary's shoulders. "Listen, Donald. Instead of trying to trap him, why don't you help him! He'll get you back on the police force, I know. And it won't be through treachery to the man who hires you!"

Donald's face flushed. "I don't like that word, Pat!"

"I don't like the fact! And I tell you I won't do it! I won't swear to the blood sample, and I won't tell about feeling his arm where it was wounded! Oh, I think it's mean and selfish to try to trap him when he's devoting all his life to fighting for... for people like us! You know you're safe! He wouldn't hurt you, Donald, no matter if you were going to shoot him down the next minute!"

Leary laughed harshly. "A lot you know about it! Any guy that's killed two hundred men will do anything if he's in a jam! All right, I'll get him without your help! Modoc O'Malley will testify to the blood, and I'll get the bullet evidence. Then we'll see! You'll be proud of me, Patsy!"

He started toward the door. "I'll—I'll *hate* you!" the girl stormed. "I'll—I'll never speak to you again! Trying to trap a nice man like Mr. Wentworth! He's probably lying wounded right now, over there in New Jersey somewhere. And all because he's tried to help people like us! Oh, Donald—"

Donald Leary was gone. Patricia Barnes dropped down on the davenport and cried. Her mother's voice whined at her from the next room. For a long time, Patricia didn't answer. When she sat up again, her eyes were reddened from crying, but her chin was set. If Richard Wentworth ever returned from that awful place in New Jersey, she'd warn him! It was her fault that Donald had begun this, but he mustn't go on with it now! He couldn't!

"Yes, mother," she said slowly. "I'm coming."

Donald probably would never speak to her again, but she couldn't help it. Richard Wentworth was terribly… nice.

RICHARD WENTWORTH was surprised that he was still alive. The realization came over him hazily when he heard a voice and recognized it as his own. He was answering someone's questions….

"I have no evidence," his own voice replied. "Satan could be Modoc O'Malley or Samuel Marco—I don't know which."

He tried to stop his voice and the words blurred a little. The struggle to assert his will forced his eyes open and he became conscious of other things. Overhead, gaunt log rafters formed a peak.

"He's coming around, chief," a voice said. "Should I give him another whiff?"

There was no answer and Wentworth, by a gigantic effort, rolled his head. It throbbed violently and his eyes were hard to focus. The walls of the room were logs, too. The furniture was crude, and the only light was oil lamps. Night pressed blackly against the windows.

Around the room were a half-dozen men, some in chairs. One stood directly over Wentworth, and his eyes were narrow with hatred. Across the cabin, Wentworth's gaze abruptly centered on a woman, supine upon a couch. Nita! For a moment, fear thudded shatteringly in his breast. She looked so... *lifeless.*

Wentworth tried to thrust himself erect, though his wrists were bound painfully before him. A hand twisted into his hair and banged his aching head down.

"What'll we do with him now, chief?" the man asked.

This question, like the one before, remained unanswered. Wentworth forced himself to calmness. Nita had only been overcome, like himself, by the narcotic gas. It had to be that. He studied in turn the half-dozen men in the room. Patently, none of these was the leader and yet, damn it, he could *feel* the baleful influence of the man called Satan!

Well, the Spider had been hoping for this, hadn't he—to fall in with some of Satan's men so he could force the truth from them? It was typical of the Spider that, hopeless prisoner that he was, his thoughts were of attack rather than fear. If he could turn the tables upon these men in some way, he might extract valuable secrets—might learn some way to avert the seemingly inevitable union of the powerful racket mobs under this emperor from hell!

"You have a coward for a leader," Wentworth said distinctly. "Even when I am bound, he doesn't dare to face me!"

He saw blood drain from the face of the killer who bent over him, heard other men start to their feet in fear. It was obvious they were in mortal terror of the man they served. Then joy surged through Wentworth, for he heard Nita's clear voice speak. She, too, had recovered from the effect of the narcotic gas.

"His type always hides behind others," Nita said. "Surely, Dick, you are not surprised?"

The man who stood over Wentworth struck him viciously in the face. The blow cut his lips, and the salty sting of blood was in his mouth.

"Keep quiet, you fool!" the man hissed. *"He* might get sore and bump us all!"

Wentworth smiled slightly, despite his puffing lips. "You are fools to serve under such a lunatic," he said. "Even Knucks Murray wouldn't behave that way. Satan is a maniac."

Frantically, the man seized Wentworth by the throat to strangle his words. Wentworth used that grip as a pivot and swung up his doubled legs with vicious force. His knees struck the man on jaw and temple, hurled him to the floor. Wentworth staggered to his feet, lifted his bound wrists and spat blood on the bonds.

"Come on, Satan," he cried mockingly, "if you are not afraid! *Abracadabra!* Appear before me, Satan!"

The man he had felled was scrambling to his feet when a

geyser of flame spurted from the floor near a curtained doorway, and the odor of sulphur filled the cabin!

Wentworth shielded his eyes with uplifted hands against the dazzling light, and saw the figure in glittering scarlet slide out from behind the curtain, taking his stand where the flames had darted upward. Also, Wentworth once more wet his wrist bonds with the blood from his lips. He had no doubt at all as to what fate was reserved for him. The white death-dust would be blown into his face! It was against that certainty that he laid his plans. WENTWORTH KNEW the thing should strike him as humorous—that one man could intimidate the worst killers that New York had ever known by such mummery as this. Laughter pumped up in his throat, but did not come out. The eyes of the creature were on him, glinting and venomous. The man himself might be a mummer, but he had killed thousands of human beings on this very day!

"Who summons Satan in mockery... *dies!*" Satan said.

Wentworth laughed, though all his body was taut. "Nice of you to come when I call, Satan," he said coolly. "If I had known you were so obedient, I might have saved myself a lot of trouble looking for you!"

Satan did not speak. His eyes remained steadily on Wentworth's face and, with a gesture, he indicated that Nita was to be brought beside him. Nita's hands were bound also, but she smiled bravely up into Wentworth's face.

"Why didn't you tell me you were studying sorcery, Dick?" she asked. "Fancy being able to evoke a spirit from hell!" Her face was pale, and the stiffness of her lips barely concealed their tremor.

Wentworth was watching the face before him with intent eyes. Plainly, Satan wore such a mask as he himself had stripped from one of the robbers of the armored car. Wentworth tried in vain to envision the face behind that mask. It was too distorted. He continued the badinage with Nita. At the last moment he could thrust her aside. Only a small quantity of the death-dust had been used to exterminate Knucks Murray, he remembered, and others in the room had not been harmed.

Wentworth was aware of the breathless waiting of the men behind him. Satan would be forced to act against him now—or his men would doubt Satan's powers! That was what Wentworth wanted.

"You have courage, Wentworth," came the harsh, forced voice of Satan. "Or else you are a fool. It does not matter which. My work is nearly done. Tonight I strip Elizabeth Junction clean. Tomorrow I shall seize the last big racket in New York and the city will belong to me—to milk as long as I wish! But this does not really interest you, Wentworth, since you won't be here to see it. Nita, come to me."

Wentworth's breath leaped high into his lungs, and he felt Nita sway toward him. This was something he had not counted on. With Nita close beside Satan, his own plans might be futile. And he had to win now. He had to... He had known, of course, that Satan would plan new depredations—but Elizabeth Junction! Fifty thousand persons lived there, and if this horror were loosed upon them....

"Nita!" Satan rasped, peremptorily. "Come here, or you shall die with this fool!"

Nita sucked in a slow breath.

"I prefer that," she said, though her voice broke. "I prefer dying with him to any existence without him!"

Satan laughed, a harsh, grating sound, and made a peremptory gesture. Nita tried to hold close against Wentworth, but the minions of Satan seized her.

"Go," Wentworth whispered without moving his lips. "I have a plan."

Nita still struggled. She didn't believe him, of course. Surely, she must realize that he would not die and leave her prisoner of this fiend? She was helpless in the hands of the men who dragged her away, and Wentworth stood very straight, head thrown back and mockery in his eyes.

"Do your best, Satan," he said clearly. "I know you now! I've left records behind which will lead straight to you. I was a fool not to realize it sooner."

Satan laughed once more and the sound was not human. The senseless cruelty in it ran coldness up Wentworth's spine. Damn it, the man *was* mad.

"A vain trick, Wentworth," he said harshly. "You told all that you knew while you slept under my gas—and it is precisely nothing. Therefore, Wentworth, you die! Watch well, Nita! This punishment awaits you if ever you... *disobey* me!"

Wentworth was taut in every muscle. He caught a breath, held it. He could resist taking any of the death-powder into his lungs, but God alone knew if it would enter his nostrils—and eyes! That powerful anhydride would turn into a deep-burning acid the instant it touched moisture. He smiled with taut lips, mockingly.

A snarl twisted the face of Satan. He whipped up a cupped palm and now blew across it, sent the terrible white death-dust swirling straight toward Wentworth's face!

CHAPTER 9
FLIGHT FOR LIFE

IT WAS exactly what Wentworth desperately had counted on—that puff of the powder directly into his face. He was ready and, as the whirling white dust mushroomed toward him, he thrust his hands into the midst of that deadly cloud, ducked his head and dived at Satan!

His eyes were tightly closed, his breath stopped in his throat, lips pressed in upon one another. He had leaped before the dust had a chance to spread. He hoped it was in time. He felt the burning bite of stuff on his wrists, which he sprayed when he spat his blood upon the ropes. He was counting heavily on the chemical affinity of anhydride for water. Dust particles should gather thickly on those wet bonds, and then....

His head drove into Satan's face and, together, they catapulted back against the wall. Nita's cry was mingled with the shouts of the men who held her prisoner. No need to tell her to struggle. But Satan... Wentworth rolled free of the man, wrenched furiously at his rope bonds. The burning at his wrists was acute. If the death-dust was doing the same thing to his ropes... Now, *they had broken!*

Like a flash, Wentworth seized Satan, unconscious from the terrific impact of Wentworth's head against his jaw. Wentworth heaved him to his feet, crouched behind him and groped for the pouch from which he had seen Satan scoop the death-dust.

"Stand, every one of you!" Wentworth shouted. "Stand still, or I'll cover you with... *the death-powder!*"

It was an empty threat, of course. He hoped the men would not realize that he could not throw the death-dust while Nita was in their midst. The men were pressed back against the walls in terror and, in the middle of the room, the cloud of death-dust that had been intended for Wentworth's face hung tenuously. Abruptly, one of the men darted to the door, wrenched it open, and plunged out.

Nita was struggling again. She got one arm free from a frightened man who was lunging toward the door. With the *jiu-jitsu* Wentworth had taught her, she hurled her other captor half across the room. He cried out in a shrill scream that rose agonizingly as he fought to recover his balance. Nita darted outside, and the man spun crazily into the midst of the floating white cloud. His scream soared and, with the sound, the other men broke in panic for the door. Wentworth flung powder after them, leaped backward into the curtained alcove from which Satan had sprung, carrying the unconscious man with him.

Violently, he ripped down the curtain and lunged on, through a narrow kitchen, against a door. Glass crashed, wood splintered, and he hurtled out into the blackness of night with his prisoner.

It was the work of instants to bind him helpless with the cloth. His fumbling hands found a hidden holster, a gun.

"To me, Nita!" he called clearly. "To me!"

Gun flashes answered him from three scattered spots, but Wentworth held his fire. He could not shoot until he knew Nita's whereabouts. He thought she would be able to elude the men who had fled in terror from the dust. Inside the building, men were screaming. It seemed to him there were three voices—which meant three guns outside.

EXCEPT WHERE the light from within spilled through the windows, the night was utterly dark; without sound save for the screams and the autumn wind that moaned through the trees and rattled their dead branches. He glimpsed movement in the shadows up the grade above him and the gun swiveled that way. Was it Nita or the killers? He had no way of knowing, but an overwhelming satisfaction gripped him. Under his knee now, Satan himself was a prisoner—and three of the six henchmen were dead. Victory was within his grasp!

Wentworth strained his eyes to make out the lines of the figure creeping toward him—then suddenly he heard Nita scream! She was a hundred feet away, up among the black trees! Without a second's delay, Wentworth squeezed the trigger of his already leveled gun. The bursting spear of powder flame showed him his target, the white face of a crouching man. He saw the man hammered backward by his lead, and then darkness closed in again.

A gun blazed up on the slope where Nita had cried, and the lead searched the air near Wentworth's head. He heard its hoarse whine, but did not answer it. He dragged Satan close against the base of a tree, used his belt to fasten the man's feet to the trunk. The body was still limp, unconscious… Up on the slope, Nita gasped in pain!

Madness raced through Wentworth. He knew what they were doing up there, all right—torturing Nita to draw him into a trap. But he did not hesitate. He backed off from the body of Satan and coolly leveled the revolver. He squeezed the trigger, hurled himself backward as lead once more whipped through the air nearby. There was grimness about Wentworth's lips as he crept up the hill. He had not killed Satan, merely made sure Satan would not escape, by putting a bullet right through the flesh of his thigh!

Once more, he heard Nita cry out, a strangled gasp! God, what were they doing to her up there in the darkness! Yet Wentworth dared not dash wildly up the slope as he longed to do. If he were careless and allowed himself to be wounded, Nita would undergo worse than that! Leaves rustled under his feet, despite his efforts. A twig cracked dryly, and once more gun flame lashed out at him!

Still, Wentworth held his fire. With a curse on his lips, he sprang up the hillside. He was careless now of noise. Let them shoot at him in the darkness! The sound that his feet made would be so loud as to confuse distance. He sprang from side to side. Twice he collided with the trunks of trees and was hurled, half-stunned, to earth. Three times, lead burned through the darkness toward him, but always missed. He must be near to Nita now, though the gun seemed always the same distance away. The devil! Were they retreating up the hill, carrying Nita with them?

The battle in absolute darkness took on the qualities of a nightmare. Trees rose ghostly before his eyes, and shrubs tripped him with the fiendishness of carefully laid snares. And ever before him, like some swamp will-o'-the-wisp, were those gun stabs and the cries of Nita. He threw a glance behind him. The cabin's lights still shone mockingly in the darkness—like homely farmhouse windows that would welcome a traveler in the night.

Wentworth's breath came dryly through his parted lips. Death lurked here on this hillside, death for Nita and himself. If he were slain, Satan would escape, and Elizabeth Junction was doomed… He forced himself to calmness, began once more his deliberate advance. He had almost reached the spot now where it seemed to him the first shots had been fired. His senses were keenly attuned. If there was to be an ambush, it would be here….

HIS EARS caught the faint metallic click on his left, and his gun smashed out flame and sound an instant before the shot spewed at him from the shrubs. A body thrashed furiously in those shrubs. A choked oath, then a dying scramble of sound. Wentworth lifted his own voice, hoarse in disguise.

"I got the louse!" he cried. "Let's find the chief!"

He stalked carelessly about in the bushes. With swift hands, he searched the body of the man he had slain. The gun had been thrown off into the darkness somewhere. He struck a match, shielding it with his hands.

"Got him right through the belly!" he yelled again.

"Okay, okay!" came the answer from up the hill. "Quit bragging and help me handle this hellcat."

Wentworth smiled thinly and started trudging up the hill. His gun, against his hip, was tight in his fist. His forearm ached from tension. He must not kill this man. It might be hard to persuade Satan to talk, and until he could find the hideout of Satan's men, and their supply of the death-powder, he had really accomplished nothing. The criminals might not strike with the same efficacy without their leader, but the powder was too deadly; they would kill too many hundreds even in their bungling attempts to imitate their leader.

"Hurry up!" the man snarled from above.

"Show a light!" Wentworth grumbled back at him.

"Show a light?" the man shouted. "How can I, you fool? I've got to hold this witch!"

The voice accomplished all that Wentworth could have hoped for from the light. He ran lightly forward. Vaguely, he could make out lurching figures in the darkness. He heard Nita gasping in her struggles, and his hand shot out. He seized her captor by the collar of his coat, and the gun in his right hand swung in a short, fierce arc.

"It's all right, darling," Wentworth said quietly.

Instantly, Nita was in his arms. "Oh, Dick! Dick!" she gasped. "I thought that beast had killed you!"

Wentworth laughed softly as his arms closed around Nita. "We've won!" he said easily. "Wait until I tie up this man, then we'll go down and make Satan talk. After that, it will be easy."

With deft movements, he stripped off the man's belt and

lashed his hands, knotting his shoe strings together. He heaved the limp body over his shoulder and, Nita beside him, made his way rapidly down the hill.

"Nothing to fear," he said. "They're all dead. Three in the woods and three in the cabin—"

"No!" Nita said sharply. "Only two in the cabin!"

An involuntary oath was jolted from Wentworth. He began to run down the slope. "We'll have to hurry!" he snapped. "The other man may have got to Satan, and... No, *there* he is!"

From the angle they approached, streaming light from the cabin window caught iridescent gleams on the scarlet scales of the recumbent figure. Yet, Wentworth frowned as he approached. Surely the man should have recovered consciousness by this time! That shot could not possibly have done any serious harm. In fact, the pain of it should have helped to revive Satan.

"Wait here," Wentworth said curtly to Nita. He advanced more cautiously, still carrying the body of the thug.

When he was a yard from Satan, his foot caught on something that was like a cord. What Wentworth did then was by instinct. He heaved the body on his shoulder directly at the figure of Satan and, as he did so, there was a muffled blast! He saw short spears of flame stab upward, then the unconscious gunman's body blotted out his view. Wentworth hurled himself backward, rolled rapidly down the hill.

"Run, Nita!" he cried. "The death-dust!"

Afterward, they crouched in the darkness and watched the dance of the motes across the lights from the cabin, and it was a half-hour before Wentworth cautiously advanced again toward the spot. He knew, without question, that this trap—a bomb of the death-powder—had been deliberately set for him with Satan's body as the bait. Yet he could not conceive of the lone surviving gunman having done such a thing. He thought of one answer which he was reluctant to accept.

His lips were thin with doubt, when finally he tumbled aside the gunman he had captured, dead now from the death-dust that had been intended for Wentworth. He stared down at the body that wore the garb of Satan—and oaths suddenly swelled in his throat.

Nita moved close to his side. "What is it, Dick?" she asked swiftly.

"Satan has been too clever for me," Wentworth told her bitterly. "He was freed by the remaining gunman, who slipped down while I was coming after you and the other crooks. Satan then killed the man who freed him and left his body here to trap us when we returned. Despite what the acid has done to him, you can recognize one of the men who was in the cabin."

Nita shuddered. "I believe their leader really is Satan!" she whispered. "Killing a man who had freed him, just to leave a trap for you!"

Wentworth's arm tightened about her. "We have no time to lose," he said, and led her rapidly through the woods. "Satan didn't delay to make sure of our deaths. That means he's hurrying to Elizabeth Junction. Fifty thousand people there, and if he looses that hellish death-dust on them, God alone knows how many thousands will perish!"

Nita said brokenly, "Heaven grant that we get there in time!"

CHAPTER 10
MASSACRE

THE RACE through the woods seemed endless, even after Wentworth stumbled upon the rutted track that wound among the trees. The clouds of the afternoon's rain had not cleared away, but along the eastern horizon there was a frosty glitter of stars. A cold wind ran with them and made a clatter like dried bones among the skeletal trees.

Wentworth's mind flashed keenly ahead. Already, he had determined upon a course of defense for Elizabeth Junction as soon as they could reach a telephone. Abruptly, a flash of brilliant lights caught his eye.

"An automobile!" he exclaimed. "I'll run and stop it!"

Nita's warning call followed him as he crashed down into the wider roadway, and he shouted reassurance. He sprang into the middle of the road, threw up both arms. Then he began to shout, loudly.

"Police!" he cried. "Halt! Police!"

The machine screeched to a halt within a few yards of Wentworth, and three men piled from it. He caught the glint of light on their weapons and, for a moment, fear gripped him. Had he walked squarely into a trap set by Satan? Then one of the men stepped forward into the full focus of the headlights with a shotgun ready in his hands.

"So you're the police, are you?" the man drawled.

Wentworth said, pleasantly, "No, I want the police. But most people won't stop on a road at night like this. I had to make sure.

Sheriff—" he hazarded a guess at the man's identity—"you heard what happened to Mill Town this afternoon?"

The man nodded dourly and kept the shotgun ready. "Reckon I did," he admitted.

"Well the same thing threatens Elizabeth Junction tonight," Wentworth said. "I've got to get to a telephone to warn them!"

Nita made a noisy descent of the last steep embankment, and the sheriff's gun swung that way. But she stepped out into the light. Her stockings were torn and there were jagged rips into her fashionable sport coat. Hair sprawled out rebelliously from under a close hat, but the smile on her lips was warm as she hurried toward the sheriff.

"Oh, thank heavens, you're here, Sheriff!" she cried. "I don't know what we would have done without you. Honest, I could kiss you!"

Wentworth masked the smile that twitched at his lips. Nita's blandishment accomplished what even long explanations on his own account could not. She poured out the story of their captivity.

The man with the shotgun rubbed his unshaven chin. "Reckon we better get to a telephone quick. Rafe, you stay here until we get back."

The car took the road at a pace impossible to a driver inexperienced in country driving. Each lunge threatened to hurl it into the ditch, but the driver handled it nonchalantly, even twisted his head about to throw questions at Wentworth and

Nita. When they reached a telephone, Wentworth hurried ahead to the instrument.

"I'll have to work this through the New York police," he said rapidly. "I'm afraid they wouldn't listen to me in Elizabeth Junction." In remarkably quick time, the call went through to Commissioner Kirkpatrick.

"Kirk?" he snapped. "Satan is moving in on Elizabeth Junction tonight. Maybe this time you'll believe my warning! All right, Kirk. I got this from Satan himself. Nita and I were taken prisoners and escaped. So did Satan. Where…?"

He twisted his head about toward the sheriff, who spat deliberately into the cuspidor. "Maraucus," he grunted. "Near Port Jervis!"

Wentworth relayed that to Kirkpatrick. "Now, listen, Kirk, this won't be an acid attack tonight because there's no rain. I figure he'll release the dust itself, which is an anhydride. The only chance Elizabeth has is to equip as many people as possible with gas masks and scatter big vats of a neutralizing base all over the town. Soft soap or even ordinary household soap will probably do. If there is an attack, any person near the scene will have to work up a lather with this soap and rub it into his eyes and breathe it down into his lungs. I'm calling you because I'm sure they won't listen to me. I'm going directly there myself. What?… Well, I wish him luck. He'll need it."

He slammed up the receiver and spun toward the sheriff. "Where can I rent a car? I've got to get to the nearest airport at once."

The sheriff still had the shotgun over his forearm. "Reckon

NITA VAN SLOAN

they can get along without you, Mr. Wentworth," he drawled. "Reckon they'll have to. You come on back to the woods, and we'll get all this here killing that's been done straightened out."

Wentworth smiled and shrugged, but he had no intention of remaining until he had satisfied the slow-grinding country justice. He would certainly be held until morning; bail might be difficult to arrange.

"Just as you say, Sheriff." He laughed. "There is some explaining to do...."

He started past the sheriff, and his hands shot out. One thrust the gun aside, the other clicked to the man's jaw, dropped him unconscious to the floor. Wentworth closed the door and sauntered out to the automobile, where the driver was intent on Nita's animated conversation. Wentworth caught a side-glance from Nita's eyes and knew that she had spotted his action inside. He opened the door beside the driver and struck with a dive that slammed the man against the opposite side of the car. It was the work of moments then to place him inside by the sheriff, to disable the phone, and get underway. He bore the accelerator to the floor.

"We can get a plane at Port Jervis, I think," he called above the engine roar. "That was nice teamwork, Nita."

Nita laughed and moved close beside him. "I always told you, you needed me in your business!"

WENTWORTH SETTLED to his driving. At the crossroads, he caught a direction error and swerved into the highway toward Port Jervis. He was frowning now, for he could not leave

Nita behind to bear the brunt of the anger of the men he had knocked out. To take her with him meant hurling her into the midst of a battle against the deadly forces of Satan, from which even he might not emerge alive.

"I'm going right with you, Dick," Nita said quietly, reading his thoughts as so often she did. "Don't try to get out of it. Besides, I've been worried recently—about myself! I'm almost sure somebody has been following me."

Wentworth smiled slightly, but quick apprehension sprang into his heart. He always feared for Nita and this seemed a direct threat. He remembered Satan's obvious liking for her... Wentworth shivered and Nita moved closer against his shoulder. The line of his jaw became grimmer.

Wentworth was just taxiing the rented plane down the field for a turn into the wind, when a motorcycle policeman raced onto the airport with his siren screaming. Wentworth laughed, whipped the plane about and bore straight at the man. He had no intention of running him down, but he did disconcert the policeman.

The officer twisted wildly aside and, by the time he had drawn his gun, Wentworth had lifted the plane into the air. Within an hour, even in this slow plane, they would raise the lights of Elizabeth Junction. What they would find there, he scarcely dared to think. It might be that the defense he had recommended would succeed in turning back the forces of Satan, but even so, many would be doomed.

Minutes dragged past while the patterns of lights that were cities slid past beneath them. He switched on the radio in the hope of getting some clue to happenings in Elizabeth Junction. He heard, instead, an alarm to all airports, requesting a lookout for the plane he was flying.

"Richard Wentworth and Nita van Sloan, wanted for homicide in New Jersey," the police announcer rasped, and reeled off their descriptions. Wentworth frowned. It was nothing his lawyers couldn't straighten out, but it could be damnably inconvenient. Neither he nor Nita could afford to be arrested now... He twisted the dial and caught the broadcast from Newark airport.

"Warning to all planes," the announcer ran out swiftly. "Give Elizabeth Junction a wide berth. Poison gas has been released there and is effective at unknown altitudes."

Wentworth cursed harshly. Satan had struck! It was less than an hour since he had flashed his warning to Kirkpatrick. Surely, Satan himself could not have reached Elizabeth Junction in time to be participating in the attack! But then there was no need that he should, and it was probably not part of his plans to be there. Otherwise, he would not have isolated himself in this remote part of the Jersey hills.

Wentworth eased the throttle wider and sent the plane at its top speed toward Elizabeth Junction. Within a few minutes now, they should be raising the lights of the city. His hope was still to join battle with the criminals and extort information... Ah, there was the city!

He spotted the lights, and felt the blood drain from his cheeks. The lights of other cities were hazed by smoke, but those of Elizabeth Junction's downtown district were almost invisible. He knew what was fogging them, and his heart grew heavy within him. Gas masks might avail against such a concentration of the white death-dust, but people would only drown themselves with soap lather before they could absorb enough to neutralize all that dust!

NEVERTHELESS, WENTWORTH grimly slanted his plane downward toward a factory yard he knew of on the outskirts of the city. He had flares, and could negotiate the landing all right—if the dust didn't get him first. The spot he had picked was on the western outskirts, and the wind would be blowing away from him toward the stricken city.

Sharply, he scanned the clouded sky as he spiraled lower. No planes there, so far as he could see. Probably this attack had been launched from ground level—and from the western, upwind outskirts toward which he was heading.

"You have a gun, Nita?" he called.

"I took a revolver from one of the officers," she replied, "but there are only five cartridges. No extras."

Wentworth was little better off, though he had fumbled a few extra rounds from the body of Satan when he had confiscated the gun. The factory, he remembered, loomed ahead. He circled over it, dropped a flare and flashed toward the earth. Moments later, he and Nita were scrambling from the ship. Now that the motor was silent, there was a deathly stillness—no rumble of traffic, no cries of people, not even the distant crack of gunfire. The wind made a faint low sound among the struts of the plane, that was all.

Wentworth and Nita gazed at each other, as they recognized

the full meaning of that silence. They had come too late. Wentworth peered about and could see, from the blackened deadness of the grass, wet from the recent rain, that death already had passed this way. The acrid bite of acid was in the air. In the street nearby, a car was jammed against a lamppost, and a man's body lay limply across the wheel. It was a terrible scene.

"There is nothing we can do here, Dick," Nita said with a curious flatness in her voice. "It will be hours before we can work our way into the city proper."

"There's just one chance," Wentworth's voice rasped. "We can try to intercept Satan's men when they retreat. They're bound to go back to New York, and it's possible the police aren't on the lookout for that. We'll see if that wrecked car over there can be operated. It doesn't seem badly broken up. And that poor fellow… won't be needing it."

It was three quarters of an hour later that they drew near the Holland Tunnel and found traffic in a hopeless tangle. Police were shooting cars into side-lanes, toward the ferries, the uptown tunnel and bridge. A huge, red-letter sign announced that the Holland Tunnel was closed, and Nita's hand went to Wentworth's. Here, too, they were late. Satan and his men, bearing with them the fruit of their slaughter, had gone on into New York City itself.

To Wentworth, that fact was ominous in the extreme. In a single day, Satan had devastated two cities in New Jersey. He had sent his death seeping through an apartment building in New York City—and now the mob was returning to Manhattan. Did that mean the terror was to be let loose upon those teeming

103

millions! Impossible to interpret affairs in any other way. And he was as much at a loss as ever—with no clue which might point the way to the guilty man.

Briefly the memory of the threat to Nita, apparent in her being followed, recurred to him. God, he could not allow her to be harmed, nor use her as bait for a trap. Nita too often had barely escaped death in his battles....

A weariness that was more than physical fatigue dragged at Wentworth. He had failed on every count, and Satan had performed his massacres unchecked. True, Wentworth had prevented what might have been a complete extermination of Maraucus, by shooting down the planes which were spreading the white death. He had also killed numbers of Satan's men. But toward the principle goal, he had made no progress at all.

Bitterly, he blamed himself for not sending a bullet through the heart of Satan while he had the man prisoner. But even that would not have stopped the slaughter in Elizabeth Junction, he was compelled to admit; nor would it have checked the further horrors that were in store.

SOON AFTER crossing on a ferry, Wentworth left the damaged machine he drove and made some phone calls. He set his lawyers to work on the New Jersey charges against him, then phoned Kirkpatrick.

"If you haven't received it already, Kirk," he said heavily, "there will be a fugitive warrant for me out in New Jersey. I didn't have time to explain before, but I was taken prisoner by Satan's men." He went on to explain the case. "I shot Satan through the left thigh. That may help to identify him!"

Kirkpatrick's voice crackled over the phone. "The left thigh! By all that's holy, Dick, that's a curious coincidence! Modoc O'Malley reported to my officers, not a half hour ago, that he was waylaid on the street by thugs and that one of them shot him—*through the left thigh!* He refused to go to a hospital, and had his own physician attend him at home. As usual, he's blaming it on the Communists."

"A coincidence?" Wentworth repeated slowly, and hope was brightening his eyes. "Yes, it may be that. What about that fugitive warrant?"

"Haven't heard anything about it," Kirkpatrick told him promptly, "but at worst, you can arrange bail. Come to headquarters as soon as you can. The carnage at Elizabeth Junction was incredible. Satan broke through Holland Tunnel. Killed all the police and the occupants of dozens of cars. I'm at a standstill, and...."

"I'll be there in a half hour," Wentworth promised. With Nita in a taxi then, he sped toward his home.

Jackson opened the gates for him, and relief spread over the man's strong face. "I have some reports, sir," he said, saluting. WENTWORTH MOTIONED him into the house and, while he showered and dressed and Nita rested in a suite which always was maintained for her, Jackson made his report. Ram Singh, wounded, was in a New Jersey hospital. His injuries were not critical. Since the event of picking up Wentworth's bloodstained hat, Donald Leary had done very little.

"I've got Leary doing guard duty on the roof, sir," Jackson went on. "Patricia Barnes has been phoning at half-hour intervals all evening. And…" He checked abruptly as a buzzer sounded faintly.

"If that's Patricia Barnes, admit her," Wentworth ordered. "No one else."

He finished dressing and joined Nita in the drawing room, where Jenkyns was serving her a cocktail. There was a placidity about his ruddy old face that was for Nita alone, for it was Jenkyns' dream that someday she should be mistress of the house. He gravely proffered Wentworth a glass.

"I've prepared a light supper, sir," he said quietly. Wentworth started to shake his head and Jenkyns stiffened. "Master Richard, you will have to eat!" he said flatly.

"If Jenkyns says I have to eat, I probably do," Wentworth laughed and dropped down upon the davenport beside Nita. "I find I'm tired." He closed his eyes, and felt Nita's cool hands upon his forehead. For a moment, he forced all thought from his mind, lay supine. Then Jackson's grave voice spoke from the doorway.

"Miss Patricia Barnes to see you, sir," he said. "And there's something I want to report."

Wentworth tautened at a worried note in Jackson's voice. "The report first," he said shortly.

"I don't know whether it's important, sir," Jackson said, "but some man called on the phone and asked if Miss Nita was here. I demanded his name, and he just hung up. The operator was unable to trace the call."

Wentworth felt Nita's hand close on his arm, and once more

knew the constriction of fear upon his heart. Nita had been followed... and now this phone call!

"Thanks, Jackson," he said quietly. "It's quite clear some danger threatens Miss Nita. Guard her with your very life. You may show in Miss Barnes."

Wentworth turned to Nita, as Jackson departed. "Don't worry, darling," he said. "No one shall take you from me!"

Nita's smile was brave, but there was a dark widening of her eyes. "I never fear anything when I'm with you, Dick. But—oh, keep me with you!"

Wentworth's hands closed on hers tenderly—and Patricia Barnes was ushered in. "I'm so glad you got back safely!" she said. "I was afraid when I found my car!"

Wentworth rose, introduced her to Nita. "It was unfair to burden you with that child," he replied.

"The state police insisted on taking it in charge." Patricia Barnes was obviously nervous, hands twisting at her purse. "Please, Miss van Sloan, I mean no offense, but... could I talk to Mr. Wentworth alone?" She waited, her face pale.

Nita assented with a smile, but Wentworth waved her to her seat and led Patricia toward the French doors that gave on the terrace.

"It's something about Donald Leary, isn't it, Patricia?" he said gravely.

The girl's blue eyes lifted to his, and there was pain about her lips. "Oh, I feel like a traitor," she said, "but I have to tell you. Donald is... Donald is getting together evidence to prove that you're... the Spider!" Once she had started, the words came more easily. "He's got quite a lot already," she rushed on. "I told him it didn't matter whether you were the Spider because... because you were nice. But he won't stop, Mr. Wentworth!" Rapidly, she outlined what evidence Leary had.

Wentworth smiled, a little wearily. "It's very kind of you to warn me, Miss Barnes. I know how you love Donald and what an effort it must cost you."

He was smiling down at her with genuine warmth. He acknowledged to himself that Leary was a danger, but it was good to have the girl come to him like this. Good, when news-papers and the people in the street, for whom he fought, cried aloud for the Spider's death. Nor could he blame Leary. He was policeman-bred and, to an officer, the Spider was a criminal.

"When," he asked Patricia, "will the blow fall?"

Her eyes widened on his face. "I believe you knew it all the time," she gasped. "Oh, Donald hasn't got the rest of the evidence yet, Mr. Wentworth. Don't let him get it, please! If he did... I'd never forgive him or myself!"

Wentworth laughed. "It's practically impossible to prove an innocent man guilty," he told her.

Patricia Barnes went away hurriedly, and Wentworth returned to the supper Jenkyns had laid out. Rapidly, he told Nita all about Leary and his evidence.

Nita's face was pale. "That's... damning, Dick," she said. "If he gets any further corroboration of his evidence! Oh, Dick, send him away at once."

Wentworth kissed her lightly. "The kid has to have a job, Nita," he said. "Don't leave the house. Here you'll be safe." Nita clung to him and her eyes, wide and frightened, remained in his memory all the swift drive down to headquarters. He was more worried about Leary's activities than he was willing to admit to her.

HE WAS ushered directly to Kirkpatrick's office and found the commissioner striding excitedly up and down the floor. He seized Wentworth by the shoulders. "Dick!" he cried. *"Major Dow has found Satan!"*

Wentworth went taut. "The devil he has! Where?"

"It was Samuel Marco," Kirkpatrick went on rapidly. "Dow was forced to kill him and two other men he found with Marco. Dow, himself, is in the hospital. And Marco had the formula for this damnable death-dust on his person!"

Wentworth rubbed his forehead with a heavy hand. "I don't suppose," he said slowly, "that Major Dow, by any chance, was wounded in the thigh also?"

Kirkpatrick stared at Wentworth with frosty, narrowed eyes. "In the thigh?" he repeated softly. "Surely, you don't suspect Dow?"

Wentworth shrugged. "No more than anyone else, but certainly not Marco. Damn it, Kirk, the thing doesn't make sense. He—"

The phone whirred on Kirkpatrick's desk, and he answered it, his voice clipped, anxious. "It's Nita, Dick."

Wentworth lunged to the phone with his heart contracting painfully in his breast. He listened through a few long seconds, and once he cursed harshly.

"Tell Jackson to throw up every possible precaution around

109

the house," he directed shortly. "And, on no account, leave there! Call me here if anything further develops." He jammed the phone back into the cradle. "When was Marco killed?"

"About five minutes past twelve," Kirkpatrick said slowly. "Why?"

Wentworth glanced at his watch. "At twenty-five minutes of one, Satan called my home," he said slowly. "Unless Nita surrenders herself to him, he says, he will destroy New York! As a warning of what he can do, he says, he will give us a little sample at noon tomorrow of how it can be done. 'This time,' I'm quoting Satan, 'I'll only kill a few thousand people!'"

CHAPTER 11
SATAN'S WARNING

KIRKPATRICK RASPED out an oath with a violence that shook his whole body. "That's dastardly!" he cried. "What in the name of Heaven can we do?"

"Put a police guard around both Dow and O'Malley!" Wentworth snapped. "I would say let Nita pretend to go, and follow her, but Satan doesn't even intend to give directions until after his 'warning' tomorrow! Round up every criminal or suspected criminal in the city and throw them into jail. They won't be able to get out until after noon tomorrow. Let the radios go crazy with the news that Dow has killed Satan. Newspapers, too. Meantime, let's go to Dow and find out just why he thinks Marco was guilty."

Wentworth cut short his speech, took a sharp turn up and

down the office. "By the heavens, Kirkpatrick, this is one time when I'm absolutely stumped. I haven't found out a single clue that would point to any one man's guilt. Unless… Good God, could it be Leary?"

Wentworth's mind raced back over the details he knew about the discharged policeman, but one thing was certain. If Leary were actually Satan, then he had had someone else to pose in his stead in New Jersey today, for Leary had been under Jackson's constant surveillance.

"Let's see Dow," Wentworth said curtly, "but Kirk, for God's sake, throw a police guard around my house! All this may be camouflage to turn our attention away from there while Nita…" He broke off his words and Kirkpatrick squeezed his shoulder as he went past to the telephone.

Less than half an hour later they entered Major Dow's room at the hospital. He was propped up in bed.

"Beat you to this one, Wentworth!" he called jovially. "But I wish now I'd had some help. They put a hole in my left thigh."

Wentworth's eyes tightened a little at the words. "You're a hero, Dow," he said dryly. "We've come to sit at your feet and learn how you accomplished your wonders."

Major Dow grinned wryly. "I've been dreading this. Can't you put off your questions a little while?"

Kirkpatrick said curtly, "I'm afraid not, Major Dow."

The army officer sighed. "Well, promise to keep it from Nita van Sloan for a day or two anyway. It might help me to beat your time, Wentworth. The entire truth of the matter is… I had an anonymous tip! I have no idea from whom!"

Kirkpatrick's forehead creased in a quick frown. "What kind of a tip?"

Dow explained rapidly. A phone call had come to the Voyagers' Club and when he answered—a man's voice told him simply that Marco was trying to skip the country, on a French boat. Dow had rushed to the dock and the moment he came in sight, two men with Marco opened fire on him. Marco pulled a gun also and, when Dow had searched Marco's body, he found the formula....

WENTWORTH LISTENED to the story in silence. It was frankly told, but his suspicions of the man were far from allayed. He knew that his open courtship of Nita was in reality deadly serious with Dow—and Satan had ordered Nita to surrender! Equally, of course, Satan might be trying to point suspicion at Dow by that device.

Wentworth said, soberly, "You're still pretty much of a hero at that, Dow. Shooting it out with three men and killing all three! Quite a feat! But, Kirk, I think we ought to give the major a police guard, don't you? Satan might have friends."

Dow protested, but Kirkpatrick was insistent and, when they left, he turned to Wentworth.

"Dick," Kirkpatrick said slowly, "he could be telling the truth, or he could have framed that whole thing himself. Sent his own men to the dock with Marco, then killed them all!"

"Or," Wentworth said dryly, "Satan could have summoned him there and deliberately shot him through the thigh so that he would fall under suspicion. There's nothing conclusive."

Kirkpatrick gripped his head between his hands. "Dick, we've got to stop all this, got to, even if…" He cut off his words.

Modoc O'Malley, at his home, told a highly circumstantial story of being shot down on the street by thugs. Therefore for him, also, Kirkpatrick insisted on a guard. But if O'Malley were Satan, the guard naturally would not stop him. Kirkpatrick's broad shoulders were stooped.

"Before God, Dick," he said, "I cannot say that I believe or disbelieve either man. Satan could have wounded O'Malley to direct suspicion on him, or O'Malley could have framed the whole story to cover the wound." He turned toward Wentworth, and his face was deadly serious. "Dick," he said thickly, "there's only one thing to do if we're going to save New York from the fate of those other cities."

Wentworth turned quickly toward Kirkpatrick, and his friend's face was twisted into a bitter mask, the mouth a harsh slit.

"I'll resign as police commissioner," Kirkpatrick went on in a flat even voice. "And you and I together, Dick, we'll… *kill O'Malley and Dow!* That's not much of an assignment for the Spider, is it, Dick?"

Wentworth felt his breath catch in his throat. "Yon damned fool!" he said. "You confoundedly damned fool! Do you realize what you're saying, Kirkpatrick?"

Kirkpatrick's face swung wholly toward Wentworth, and there was a brightness in his eyes that came from tears. "Dick, Dick! We've fought a hundred battles together. You've convinced me. The Spider's way is the right way. The law is imbecilic. Confound

113

it, I can't even arrest those two men! Even though I'm convinced that one of them is Satan—O'Malley or Dow." He nodded.

"Dick, you know you're the Spider. Take my hand between yours. I'm your man from now on. We'll slaughter these beasts who commit wholesale murder. We'll give people a clean city to live in. We…" Kirkpatrick's words broke on a dry, wracking sob that he tried vainly to smother in his throat. His head sagged.

Wentworth threw an arm across Kirkpatrick's shoulders. "You're talking like a fool, Kirk," he said quietly, "and you know it. You wouldn't last two days of the Spider's life. There's no compromise in you and too much conscience. You serve your city best as you are—the best police commissioner the country has ever known! I'm really surprised at you, Kirk."

He waited.

Kirkpatrick's head came up slowly. He jerked out a handkerchief angrily and blew his nose. "Forgive me, Dick," he said, his voice still strained. "You are right, of course, and I'm dead wrong."

WENTWORTH LEANED back against the cushions, and his own face was haggard. The truth was that Kirkpatrick's words had struck close to home. Wasn't it better, he asked himself, to kill these two men, even though one of them might be innocent, rather than risk that thousands of innocents might die tomorrow? If he could be sure that it would achieve that result!

But Wentworth was remembering his doubts about Leary—and the formula had been found on Marco! Also Elizabeth Junction had been ravished when Satan had just escaped

114

captivity high up in the Jersey hills. No, Satan's mere death would not suffice. He and all his associates must be wiped out at one fell swoop!

Wentworth's lips were set in a bitter line. At a dead end, but they must find a way out, must trace down Satan and his men this night and wipe them out—or tomorrow hell would burst in all its fury over New York City!

"We might as well look at Marco," he said. "If the man was guilty, there might be something on the body that would help."

The night supervisor of the morgue shook his head when they went to him. "I didn't have any order to pick up a body on West Street," he said. "You sure it was a stiff?"

Kirkpatrick sprang to the telephone, snapped through a call to headquarters and threw curt questions, then went striding out again to his car while he explained to Wentworth.

"A correction on the first report came through," he said. "Marco wasn't killed! He's in St. Vincent's."

Wentworth caught Kirkpatrick's arm. "Are you sure?" he demanded.

Kirkpatrick stared at him blankly. "Sure? The hospital wagon took him away." Abruptly, Kirkpatrick swore and started back for the phone. "God knows I hope you're wrong, Dick. If he has made a getaway...."

They had gone only two blocks in Kirkpatrick's big official limousine when the announcer's ringing voice came to them.

"Calling Car One Hundred!"

Kirkpatrick bent rigidly forward, for "One Hundred" was the code call for his own car.

The announcer's flat, unemotional voice ran on.

"Party hasn't arrived at hospital, Car One Hundred. Investigation. That is all." Without pause, the voice clipped out a fresh order.

"Calling all cars! Calling all cars! This is a fifty signal. Fifty signal! Locate at once St. Vincent's Hospital Ambulance Number Seven…."

Wentworth and Kirkpatrick stared at each other.

"Do you want to kill Major Dow and O'Malley now?" Wentworth asked him softly.

The commissioner's voice was harsh. "I dread their finding that ambulance!"

Acting on the signal-fifty order, which took precedence over all others, the police radio cars found the ambulance. It was hidden where shadows were dark beside the loading platform of a West Side warehouse. The intern and inside police guard were dead, killed by the death-dust of Satan. The driver was huddled against the brick wall with a bullet through his chest. He was able to gasp out that a car had pinned him to the curb and he had been shot before he could draw his own gun. Of what had happened afterward, he knew nothing.

Within the ambulance, there was a faint, unmistakable odor of brimstone. Marco was gone.

CHAPTER 12
HELL'S OWN

WHEN KIRKPATRICK and Wentworth reached the scene, the rising sun had already thrown its first red rays against the peaks of the skyscrapers and the city traffic was beginning to thicken. They found newspapermen there before them. The offices and the radio broadcast companies had the news of Marco's escape.

The newsmen had other information, too. "I called Major Dow to find out what he thought about it," one shrewd-faced newspaperman told Kirkpatrick. "Had a tough time getting the hospital to put the call through, but I got a friend there."

"What did Dow say?"

"Dow hit the ceiling!" the reporter chortled. "Called you some nice names, Kirkpatrick. Said he'd, by God, leave his sick bed and find Marco for you again—only this time he'd make sure Marco didn't get away."

Wentworth's eyes narrowed at the information. What the newspaperman reported was entirely in keeping with Dow's character—but, if he *were* Satan, leaving the hospital might give him an opportunity to elude his police guard! All his suspicions of Dow returned with a rush. He drew Kirkpatrick aside.

"We'd better make sure Dow doesn't escape surveillance," he whispered, "and check on O'Malley."

Kirkpatrick nodded sharply, but his phone calls arrived too late. Dow had left the hospital and there were no reports from

117

the officers assigned to guard him. O'Malley also had left his apartment with the two men watching him.

"For a private hospital where *he* can be safe from assassins," his manservant reported. "No, sir, he didn't say what hospital."

Kirkpatrick whirled fiercely on Wentworth. "We should have put them out of the picture while we had them pinned down," he said sharply.

Wentworth's face was set and hard. Impossible to determine which of these men had acted in good faith and which was Satan himself—Marco, Dow or O'Malley. It was nearly seven o'clock. Within five hours, Satan had promised to devastate Manhattan. Wentworth beat his temples with his knuckles. Damn it, there had to be a way out of this, to find and destroy Satan and his men.

Abruptly, his head jerked up. "Kirkpatrick," he asked quickly, "can you arrange for a civic organization to award some medals, at quarter of twelve today—to Major Dow for his recovery of the formula; to Modoc O'Malley for pointing the finger of suspicion at Marco, in the first place? Arrange for it to be done on the steps of city hall. Publicize it in the newspapers. Dow and O'Malley won't dare to miss that. We'll have to depend on your men to find and return Marco—if we can't do it ourselves. And, at quarter of twelve, I'll point out Satan to you!"

Kirkpatrick seized Wentworth by the shoulders.

"Don't quibble, man!" he said sharply. "If you know who Satan is...."

Wentworth shook his head impatiently. "I didn't say I knew! I could guess, but such evidence as there is can be read too many

118

ways to be sure. I said I'd point him out—and I will! But meantime, we've got to get Marco! Will you arrange for the medals!" He waited for a reply.

Kirkpatrick eyed him steadily through a long moment. "Dick, you realize how much hinges on this! If we fail… If none of these men is guilty—and that's impossible, God knows—we're doing nothing at all to prevent the destruction of the city."

Wentworth's lips twisted in a strained grin. "There is always… Nita," he said harshly.

Kirkpatrick stiffened. "Good God, Dick, you wouldn't let Nita… go?"

Wentworth said nothing. His face was absolutely without color, but there was no wavering in his gaze.

Kirkpatrick said, violently, "Dick, you're not human!" He turned jerkily away and strode toward his limousine.

Wentworth followed. "If you'll take me to headquarters," he said heavily, "I'll get my car. I have work to do."

Kirkpatrick threw an order at the driver and sat bolt upright while the car wove through traffic. From time to time, he glanced at Wentworth but it was not until they reached headquarters that he finally burst out.

"You surely don't have any idea that Satan would keep his word, even if Nita did surrender to him! Or do you have some fantastic idea about being able to follow Nita and trap Satan? You can be sure he'll be watching for that and that he'll effectively eliminate anyone who follows her—with the death-dust!"

Wentworth climbed stiffly from the car. "You'll have the civic organization offer the medal, Kirk. Get some sort of platform

Dying men were crawling the floor as the machine gun

in Wentworth's hands chattered away!

rigged and arrange for a broadcast. I want to make the presentation speech myself."

Kirkpatrick caught Wentworth's arm, and Wentworth wrenched free. "For God's sake, Kirk," he said harshly. "Do you think the prospect gives me any pleasure, or that I don't know what a slim chance it would be? Do you think that you or I, or the entire police force, could prevent Nita from going if she thought she could save the city? I've arranged for every telephone call that enters the house to be traced immediately. I've thrown up every defense I can think of, and they won't be enough! Damn it, you know they won't be enough!"

Wentworth got hold of himself by a strenuous effort. His breath was making harsh sounds through his nostrils. Kirkpatrick said slowly, "Forgive me, Dick. I'll do all I can to help you." **THEIR HANDS** locked in a clasp that clung, then Wentworth turned sharply away to his car, flung into the driver's seat. He had been very bold in his statement to Kirkpatrick, but was far from sure of the results. What he had in mind was an effort to frighten one of the men so that he betrayed himself. He had his own theories of the mentality of the man who could conceive of such an impersonation as Satan and ruthlessly destroy so many thousands of lives for his own greed. If that theory was wrong, all his plans would fail. If it was right… Damn it, he had to be right!

Nita ran into his arms when he entered his home again. Smudged shadows beneath her violet eyes told how dreadful the night had been for her.

"I'm going to go, Dick!" she said. "I have to! Can't you see, my life isn't worth the sacrifice of all the thousands…."

Wentworth kissed her softly, "Yes, dear," he said. "I knew that would be your decision. If it's humanly possible, I'm going to make it unnecessary for you to go. But if you do go... I'll have a way of tracing you." He raised his voice. "Jackson, call Leary and come yourself."

When Leary entered, Wentworth faced the two men with his arm about Nita and told them quietly of Satan's demand. He saw Jackson's jaws knot with anger and the color drain from Leary's face.

"That's monstrous!" Leary said violently.

Wentworth looked straight into the man's eyes. He could not dislike Leary, and he knew he could be trusted for the assignment he was about to give him. He *had* to trust Leary.

"Leary," he said slowly, "sooner or later, Satan is going to notify Miss van Sloan of what she must do. When she leaves here, you will follow her. I don't need to tell you how important it is that you should not lose sight of her. And I don't need to tell you also that Satan will expect you or someone to follow and will plan to kill you.

"Will you accept the assignment?"

Jackson stepped forward with blood angrily red in his temples and throat. "In what way have I failed you, Major?" he demanded harshly. "When have I lost your confidence? That's my job, to take care of Miss Nita. If you can't trust me... If Miss Nita...."

Wentworth smiled, and his eyes were kindly. "I have other work for you, Jackson, which Leary cannot perform."

Jackson saluted with a vibrant snap of his arm, stepped back again.

Leary's jaw was set. "I'll take that assignment, sir," he said. "I couldn't fail you, Miss van Sloan, when you... when you're doing what you are."

Wentworth nodded. "Protect her with your life, Leary, but remember it's more important to find where she's being taken, than anything else. As soon as we've made certain provisions, you and Miss van Sloan will hide in the back of a car, which Jackson will drive from here. You will go to Miss van Sloan's apartments, and I'll arrange for phone calls to be relayed there by the phone company. In this way, when she starts out in answer to Satan's summons, you will escape any watch that may be kept over this mansion. I hope you will. But you will observe all possible precautions, nevertheless. Dismissed, Leary. Rest, until you are summoned by Miss van Sloan. Jackson, you are going to help me trap Satan...."

It was nine o'clock when Wentworth finished his instructions to Jackson and was ready to leave again. He took Nita in his arms again.

"I'm going to try to make it unnecessary for this set-up to be used," he told her softly. "There's just a chance that a lead I have may take me to Satan and his headquarters. If that fails, it will be up to you. It seems to me my plans for Jackson and the presentation speech at city hall are—difficult to bring off."

Nita's arms were tightly about his neck, and there was a rich smile on her lips. "Dick," she whispered. "Dick, if anything should happen...."

"Not to you, dearest!" Wentworth said fiercely. He strained

her to him. "God wouldn't let anything happen to anyone as brave, as sweet...."

Nita covered his lips with her palm. "Goodbye, Dick," she said softly.

"Not goodbye. Never... say goodbye."

Nita was standing straight and still in the middle of the drawing room when Wentworth left her but, as soon as he was gone, the stiffness went out of her. She crumpled on the davenport and ground her knuckles against her lips.

"Make me brave," she whispered. "Oh, make me *brave!*"

WENTWORTH HURLED his coupé through the streets with a fierceness that was perilous, and blocks passed before he could force himself to drive quietly. Fears and doubts shook him. He had told Nita he had a lead, but it could scarcely be called that.

He was going to the apartment building where everyone had been killed by death-dust during his absence in New Jersey. Police had been unable to discover how the dust had been spread through the building so swiftly and completely. He had a theory about that, and if it worked out...! God, he should have heeded Kirkpatrick's plea the night before and wiped out every possible suspect. Better that than the fate that hung over the city—over Nita—if he failed! His plans seemed good, but so many things could wreck them, and wreckage meant—disaster!

Kirkpatrick was waiting for Wentworth at the apartment building.

"I've arranged the medals," Kirkpatrick said curtly. "Radio

and newspapers are carrying the word. Every man on the force is hunting for Marco. Will you have Leary on hand, too?"

Wentworth's lips moved stiffly. "I hope so," he said, and did not explain. But if Leary were not there, it was likely Wentworth would not be there either! Nita… He must put her from his mind, or he could not think.

"As I understand it," he said, in a voice devoid of expression, "there was one apartment from which people escaped. They died in the halls afterward."

Kirkpatrick nodded. "I've got the day-men here—the building employees who were off duty at the time."

Wentworth strode toward the men. "Would any of you receive complaints if an apartment were cold—if there weren't enough heat?"

One of the men nodded jerkily. "I did," he said. "Apartment Eleven-C complained just yesterday, a little while before I went off and this thing happened."

Kirkpatrick uttered a sharp exclamation. "That's the apartment from which the people escaped. You mean, the heating system…."

Wentworth strode through the open door of an apartment and bent over the steam valve. When he looked up, he was smiling thinly, and Kirkpatrick swore under his breath. The vent of the steam valve was enlarged to many times its normal size and the edges were irregular, as if eaten by a powerful acid!

"By the heavens, Dick," Kirkpatrick exclaimed. "You've hit it! This building is one of the few apartments that get their heat from the steam company* instead of having a furnace of its own! How in the name of Heaven did you hit on that, Dick?"

Wentworth shrugged. "I couldn't think of anything else that would give access to every room in the building at approximately the same time. What we've got to find now is where the steam pipes were tapped. My guess would be that it was from the tunnels under the streets through which the steam pipes run. If you will remember, the men who robbed the armored truck escaped by under-street tunnels... By the way, Kirk, this place isn't terribly far from the spot where Marco was taken from the ambulance!"

Kirkpatrick's eyes were flashing as he strode toward the door. "Get men from the steam company here at once. An emergency!" he barked at a police sergeant. "We want men who know the tunnels. They are to bring equipment for opening them, together with blueprints of the tunnels' courses. And it's got to be fast!"

"We won't wait!" Wentworth urged. "There might be a leak that would alarm them!"

Kirkpatrick peered at him, knuckled his military mustache.

---

* Author's Note: In New York City, many office buildings do not have furnaces, but buy their steam, metered like gas or electricity, from a utility company. This company has steam pipes running beneath the city streets from central plants, and access is had to them by man-holes and tunnels through which workers can walk to make repairs or to regulate the flow of steam. A few of the larger hotels and apartment buildings also are similarly supplied.

"I don't understand, Dick. You mean you expect to find a hideout of the gang?"

"Think, man!" Wentworth cried. "It may not mean anything, but that robbery of the armored truck was no more than three blocks from here. Four blocks in the opposite direction is the spot where Marco's ambulance was hijacked. Two blocks down—almost halfway between those two—is the place where Marco was shot. And now this apartment building. It's all in the same radius. It looks to me as if there might be an operating headquarters nearby. Whether it is underground, or in some structure that can be reached from the tunnels, I don't know. We can't risk it! Throw a cordon around the entire district, open manholes and put police guards underground! We have nothing to lose!"

Kirkpatrick sprang into action. Organization was his special attribute and, within minutes, he had the cordon mapped and the forces in motion. A call brought an emergency wagon at top speed. Its gas masks were quickly distributed after the manhole was opened. Gun in hand, Wentworth climbed rapidly down into the steam-tunnel beneath the street and Kirkpatrick was not far behind. Within a few minutes, their powerful flashlights had spotted the steam-line tap through which the death-dust had been forced into the system of the apartment building.

Wentworth straightened and sent the beam of his light stabbing through the close darkness to the south. "Down there," he said, "is the center of all this activity."

Kirkpatrick stood just behind him in the stuffy confines of the tunnel. Beside them ran the steam pipes, telephone and electricity conduits, a gas main. Between the pipes in the narrow passageway, there was just space for a man to stand erect. It was hot.

"We're near the end, Dick." Kirkpatrick lowered his voice but even so it raised curious echoes along the tunnel. "I'm sure of it!"

Wentworth hesitated, his thoughts winging to Nita. He glanced at his watch. Ten o'clock. If he should be trapped down here, Nita would be doomed. But if he succeeded, she might never have to take the hideous risk of facing Satan alone. He took a slow stride forward, another, then went rapidly along the tunnel. It would be hard for any gunman, no matter how wild, to miss a target in this narrow way....

CHAPTER 13
DEATH BELOW!

WENTWORTH HAD not advanced fifty paces along the corridor before he checked and pointed his light at a sprinkling of white dust on the floor. It sparkled brightly.

"Unless I miss my guess," he said softly, "that is... death-dust!"

Kirkpatrick's breath sucked in sibilantly. Men strung out behind him in single file passed the word along to the surface. The dust would be gathered up cautiously by a man in a mask, tested. Wentworth's pace quickened. There was a fury of impatience in his breast. They were on the right trail, but would they arrive in time!

He began to run with long loping strides, and his light ceaselessly swept the side walls behind the masking pipes and wires.

Abruptly, he halted. There was another sprinkling of the white dust, but this time it was far in against the wall. Wentworth stooped and peered under the pipes, and his breath caught in his throat. There was no doubt of it. The wall had been recently breached, and there was no mortar between the bricks. His heart pounded hard in his chest.

"We have arrived, Kirk," he said softly. He adjusted his mask and, on his knees, worked close to the wall. Deftly, he loosened a single brick and drew it noiselessly out, peered into the darkness beyond. He could make out nothing, at first. Then, with the flash held close beside his head, he made out rough dirt walls shored with timbers and, a few yards beyond, an iron-studded door! Rapidly, he began to haul down the bricks, stacking them against the wall until he had made a passage large enough to slide his body through. He straightened then, lifted his gas mask.

"I've thrown men around the building," Kirkpatrick said quietly. "It's that old armory, abandoned by the government a long time ago. It's been used as a freight depot for trucks most recently, but, as well as I recall, it's empty now. If you'll give the men ten minutes, we'll have that building sewn up tighter than a drum, and then...."

Kirkpatrick's lips drew grimly thin. Wentworth glanced again at his watch. Half-past ten. He swore softly under his breath. It had been over an hour since he had left his car and, with it, all hope of making contact with Nita. Jackson....

A whisper ran along the line of police. The sergeant just behind Kirkpatrick stepped forward, saluting.

"Mr. Wentworth, sir," he said. "Your man, Jackson, reports that the radio signals have started!"

Wentworth thanked him in a voice that was strained in spite of himself. Kirkpatrick stared, a question in his eyes.

"That means," Wentworth said quietly, "that Nita has heard from Satan and has started to… meet him!"

"Radio signals?" Kirkpatrick asked.

Wentworth gestured abruptly. "A plan which I hope will permit me to follow her… if Satan doesn't discover it. Damn it, Kirk, I can't wait any longer. Your men should be around the armory by now."

Kirkpatrick glanced at his watch, and nodded slowly. "I'm going first!" he said and slipped his mask into place.

Before Wentworth could phrase a protest, Kirkpatrick, gun in hand, was worming his way through the breach in the wall. Wentworth was immediately behind him and, silently, they moved up to the metal door which barred their way.

Wentworth's exploring fingers discovered that the door was set solidly into a stone wall. He could find no lock or latch. Together, he and Kirkpatrick set their shoulders against the barrier and put on a slow, hard pressure. The door creaked slightly, but yielded only a fraction of an inch. By experimenting, Wentworth found that it moved inward slightly at top and bottom, but held fast in the middle.

He lifted his mask. "A bar, probably. I think I can force it." IN THE darkness, his hands went beneath his vest to a leather girdle he wore about his waist—the tool kit of the Spider. From it he fingered a thin strip of tempered steel and, with it, attacked the edge of the door. Beneath the mask, his lips smiled thinly. Here, beside the police commissioner, he was practicing the arts of the Spider!

He worked the strip through the slit where the door met jamb and, moments later, began to force it upward against the bar. He felt the bar slip from its catches, balanced it precariously on his metal tool and pushed the door open a fraction until he could catch the bar with his hand. He swung the barrier cautiously wider and… they were in the basement of the armory!

In the same instant Wentworth thrust the door wide, blinding lights blazed into his face. He flung himself flat, dragging Kirkpatrick with him, and a submachine gun began to yammer thunderously. Behind them, a policeman screamed hoarsely, and the body pitched down, writhing, across Wentworth's legs. Wentworth's guns were already in his hands, and they spoke together in a hammering roll of fire that mocked the machine gun and stitched the blackness behind the lights with bullets. The machine gun stopped….

Instantly, Wentworth was up and charging toward those lights. He could hear shouts, and somewhere a bell raised a clamoring alarm. Into the darkness, Wentworth plunged. His dazzled eyes could see nothing until he holstered a gun and sprayed light from his flash over the scene. Another stone wall barred their way—another steel door. On the floor lay the machine-gunner. A bullet had smashed his face.

Swiftly, Wentworth flung his light about. The basement way they had entered was a blind alley. Not even a flight of stairs led upward. There was no way out except that hole in the wall by which they had entered or this steel door. Without a moment's hesitation, Wentworth whipped up the machine gun and strode toward the door.

Kirkpatrick was beside him, and his voice bawled out a sharp order to the police pouring through the opening. In response to it, the men checked and drew back close against the wall, waiting. Then there was a hoarse, muffled shout as men cried out through their masks. From somewhere in the overhead darkness, white clouds of dust were whirling down upon them! No need to wonder at its purpose. This was the death-powder of Satan!

Would their masks avail against it? Wentworth did not know. He flung himself at the door. This one bore a great lock upon it, and Wentworth stepped back, pulled the muzzle of the machine gun into line and squeezed the trigger. Battering at the ancient lock, .45 caliber lead ripped it open, smashed the mechanism within. An instant of deafening gun thunder, then Wentworth seized the handle of the door, wrenched and flung it inward.

In a single, long leap, Wentworth angled through the doorway, the machine gun chattering in his hands. His targets were fifty yards away, men jamming through a doorway in the wall. A bomb arched toward him, fell short, and a cloud of white death-dust geysered upward from the floor. Other guns were banging behind him now, and men were clawing the floor there in that doorway—bodies forming a dam over which their companions could not escape!

How many already had poured out through that vent, it was impossible to guess, but there were a full dozen within. Guns hammered and leaped in their hands. Lead lashed the air around

Wentworth. He heard a coughed groan behind him, and the machine gun went dead in his hands. Wentworth dropped it, whipped out his automatics and threw himself prone. Five men remained on their feet against the distant wall. Five men... and then none at all.

WENTWORTH THREW a swift glance behind him. There were a dozen police at his back. Kirkpatrick was reeling on his feet, his left arm limp and bleeding at his side. Kirkpatrick flung his other arm into the air in a gesture that sent the police charging across the huge basement room. But Wentworth was ahead of him.

Like an arrow from a bow, he sped toward that corpse-blocked doorway. Impossible to get through until the bodies were cleared away. He worked furiously. From beyond, he caught the sound of pounding feet. There were fugitives, then. Two other men labored beside him now.

Wentworth jerked up his mask. "Upstairs, some of you!" he shouted. "Warn the tunnel guards that men are escaping that way!"

His mask still up, he clambered over the bodies in the doorway and then stopped. A man, flat on his back on the floor, lifted his hands in petition.

"Thank God you've come!" he panted. "These fiends were torturing me!"

Wentworth swore under his breath.

"Marco!" he said.

He seized the man and hauled him back into the inner room while policemen dashed past him. Marco—a prisoner as he said, or the leader of this mob? Wentworth felt his gun like a sentient thing in his hand. What did it matter? If all the suspects were killed….

Abruptly, his head whipped up. He sniffed. That odor! It was city gas from the mains! The smell of it was powerful, increasing momentarily. With a shout, he hurled himself at the doorway.

"Don't shoot!" he cried after the police in the tunnel. "Don't shoot! They've smashed a gas main! It will blow up!"

Even as the words left his lips, one of the policemen, poised in the entrance to the tunnel, was squeezing the trigger. It was too late. A blast of white-streaked crimson fire smashed out hideously behind the man's silhouetted figure, and Wentworth felt himself plucked up by the breath of a hell-born gale and hurled backward across the basement room. There was blinding light… then blackness.

SIX BLOCKS away from the spot where Wentworth had met Satan, and defeat, Jackson was bending eagerly over a radio direction-finder in Wentworth's Daimler. Into the receiver spilled a series of rhythmic dots. It meant that Nita van Sloan had started out to meet Satan.

In the lining of her fur coat and muff was rigged a shortwave broadcasting unit which operated on batteries. It was effective only a very short distance and the moment the sounds came in, Jackson sent word to Wentworth and rolled the Daimler in the direction which the finder indicated.

At Wentworth's home, Jenkyns would be operating a similar receiver, and Leary, in a car equipped like the Daimler, would be doing the same. Among the three of them, they hoped to be able, by triangulation,* to spot the place to which Nita was taken. Elation and a hard anger coursed through Jackson's veins. The system was going to work. If Miss Nita could just keep Satan from discovering the sending unit in her coat and muff, they could track her without difficulty. If there were any interruption—Jackson's large mouth closed like a steel trap—then God help Miss Nita!

He rolled the big Daimler rapidly northward, hearing the signals grow louder and louder as he sped. Several times he had to adjust the finder, which meant that Miss Nita was still in motion. When she became stationary, he would check with Jenkyns, and Leary also would phone in his findings. Then they would each mark out the course on a map of the city.

At that instant, there echoed behind Jackson a rolling, muffled explosion. Ahead of him, a manhole cover leaped into the air like a flipped coin. It smashed down on the pavement. A tongue of flame darted from the pit.

---

* AUTHOR'S NOTE: Triangulation is the method used by land stations to locate a ship at sea, a plane, or any other radio sending station. Any two receiving stations, equipped with finders, and separated from each other, can achieve this. The finder is turned until it brings in the radio broadcast at maximum strength. At this time, It will be pointing straight toward the station. The compass bearing is then taken. The two stations then plot these compass lines on a map and the point where the lines intersect will be the point from which the broadcast originates. It is also possible for a ship, keeping a beam from land at maximum intensity, to steer straight for the broadcasting station.

Jackson's face whitened. Major Wentworth was down in those tunnels! Jackson's hands faltered on the wheel, but only for a moment. Then their grip tightened again, and he pushed steadily on. There were hard corrugations in his jaw muscles. God alone knew what had happened, but his orders were to follow where the radio signals led.

"I am placing Miss Nita's life in your hands," Wentworth had said.

Jackson's lips moved in silent curses. He had to shift the finder more rapidly now. Apparently, Miss Nita was in a fast-moving car. Jackson pressed down on the accelerator and then... the signals stopped! A ripping oath burst from his lips. The stopping of the signals could mean only one thing! Satan or his men had found out about the radio broadcaster in Miss Nita's coat and had... smashed it! Jackson no longer had a way to follow her!

CHAPTER 14
NITA'S SACRIFICE

THE HOURS that Nita van Sloan waited for the summons from Satan were the longest she had ever known. More than a dozen times, she walked toward the fur coat and muff in which the radio broadcaster had been rigged. For the rest, she roamed restlessly about her studio apartment, adjusting things that did not need her touch, standing blindly before the broad windows that gave out over the Hudson.

She had three guns concealed upon her person. One, in a muff, she expected to pull at the first moment she met the men of Satan, thus preventing a search of the muff. Another, she would carry inside her right knee, fastened to her garter; a third in the bodice of her dress. She had another defense of which even Dick Wentworth knew nothing—a vial of poison that would be swift and merciful to her if everything else failed!

When the telephone rang, Nita felt all her body tauten, but her voice was cool when she spoke. Her eyes closed then, and a strong shudder raced over her body as she heard the rasping of Satan's strained and elemental voice.

"Yes," she said faintly. "Yes, I will come."

Her movements were utterly calm as she drew on the coat and small hat, picked up the muff and, with her fingers, closed the contact which started the signals. They dribbled from her own radio across the room, and thus she knew that the outfit was working. Swiftly then, she left the building.

Fifteen minutes later, walking rapidly westward on East Seventy-second Street, as she had been bidden, she saw a gray sedan swerve to the curb beside her. The chauffeur, in uniform, lifted his hat.

"Can I give you a lift, Miss van Sloan?" he asked. Mockery was upon his thin lips, a warning glitter in his eyes.

Nita drew in a deep breath and turned toward the curb. "Thank you, James," she said, and stepped into the tonneau. A man was there and, as Nita faced him, she ripped the small automatic from her muff. It was instantly twisted from her grasp, and the man laughed.

"That's no way to treat a gent that offers you a lift, Nita," the man reproved her, contorting his smooth face in a wink. He pulled her down to the seat beside him. Nita put her hands into her muff and sat very erectly, head high.

"Home, James," the man ordered. "And turn on the radio so we can see if our friends, the police, are on the trail."

A gasp squeezed up into Nita's throat, but she choked it there. As soon as that radio clicked on, the men would hear the intermittent signals of the set Dick Wentworth had rigged. They would be totally unintelligent, if they did not suspect instantly that it was in some way concerned with her kidnapping—even if its loudness did not betray the fact that it came from within the car itself!

NITA CLOSED her eyes. She could stop the signals by opening the switch within her muff, but the instant she did that all her contact with Dick and his men was broken. It was true that, presently, she might be able to turn it on again. But by that time, she might be beyond the narrow range which her sending set could cover. Dick had warned her that the signals were weak. That was why Leary and Jackson, perhaps Dick with him, were following in cars.

Nita drew in a deep, slow breath—and broke the contact! When the radio came on, the signals were dead. She was on her own now, with her guns and… and the vial of poison! It was an effort to sit erectly, hold her head proudly.

"If there's anybody on your trail, sister," the man beside her grunted, "it's going to be just too bad for them! They'll just have to take a powder—*a death-powder!*" He laughed uproariously at his own joke, and a police announcer came on the air.

Hope leaped up in Nita's heart. Firmly, she closed the switch of the radio and heard the dotted signals bubble through the voice of the announcer. They were conspicuous. But, if she only turned it on while the police announcer was speaking, the men would logically think that it was some defect in the police mechanism. Abruptly, Nita's attention was riveted on the announcer's words.

"Tunnel guards, be on your guard. The criminal known as Satan, with an undetermined number of men, is making his escape along the tunnels. They are heavily armed and have set the gas main afire. All will don gas masks at once and under no circumstances remove them. Reserves are coming to assist you. That is all."

The man beside Nita swore harshly. "You hear that, Digger?" he exclaimed. "They found out about the tunnels. Sounds like they think they got the chief stopped!"

The chauffeur called Digger opened the throttle. "Better dump this dame where the boss said and go help him, eh, Calo?"

The announcer came back before the man beside Nita could answer. Nita's heart beat fast. The gas main's on fire and Dick… She glanced at Calo's face. It still had that bland smoothness, but his eyes were tight and hard.

"Cars Seventeen, Twenty and Twenty-two, proceed at full speed to Thirty-seventh Street and Ninth Avenue." The announcer said rapidly. "Man dressed in red, believed Satan, reported coming out of manhole there. Watch for cars, with man in red, leaving neighborhood. Tunnel guards, close in toward center. Satan believed to have escaped, but his men may still be underground…."

With a hard laugh, Digger cut off the radio. "So they thought the chief was trapped, did they? We better hurry along to the hideout, or he'll be sore we're so late. Ain't you the lucky dame, Nita, having the chief soft on you!"

Nita did not answer. Her eyes peered straight ahead. So Dick had failed in his first effort, and there now was no way out for her except to face Satan and pray that the broken radio signals had been followed! They were already far north in the city, speeding toward the outskirts, and she had been able to operate the signals only at brief intervals. She allowed them to continue, since the radio was cut off. But it well—might be too late.

Nita sought within herself for the courage which rarely failed her. In her heart, she whispered Dick's name. If only she could be sure he would come! Sickening fear held her. A gas main set fire in the tunnels where Dick was chasing Satan!

Abruptly she was aware of two other cars that crawled past the one she occupied. Calo yelled through the window.

"Anybody try to follow?"

The other cars were full of Satan's men, and they yelled back a jeering assurance. "We covered four blocks on each side and a mile behind. Nobody showed."

Strangely, Calo was frowning when he leaned back once more. "Looks like your boyfriend, Wentworth, ain't taking such good care of you, Nita. We were hoping he'd try something. If he's worked out something fancy, it's going to be just too bad for him. He'll walk into about fifteen guns—that is, if he can wade through the death-powder!"

Nita sat rigidly, and did not answer. For her, after that, time

141

seemed to stand still. She was numb with horror when the car finally coasted up to a stone house, set well back from the road in a fashionable residential district. Without resistance, she allowed Calo to thrust her toward the basement entrance.

SHE WAS thrust into a room, and horror filled her throat. From a divan against the wall rose the incredible figure of the arch-murderer who had summoned her! The scarlet garb of Satan glittered as if with internal fires. Nita's shock was so great that she did not notice there was a radio in the room, or that the rhythmic dots of the apparatus she carried were sounding loudly in it.

"Welcome, my woman!" Satan said harshly. "Men, she is leading Wentworth here, if he still lives, by some sort of radio broadcast she carries on her person. I have been listening to the signals draw nearer for the last fifteen minutes. Set the trap, while I—" he laughed hoarsely—"find the apparatus!"

His hands reached out and he came steadily toward Nita. His figure seemed enormous, supernatural. A paralysis gripped her. It was only when he was within a stride of her that Nita recovered herself. With a lightning movement, she whipped the automatic from her bodice and fired point-blank at Satan's chest.

Satan laughed! He reached her in a stride and wrenched the gun from her hand. "You should have shot at the throat, my dear!" he said. "You overlooked bulletproof vests!"

His strength was immense. Without effort, he held her prisoner while his hands discovered the radio equipment and peeled off her coat. The signals still sounded, but now they meant death to Dick instead of salvation to Nita! She fought frantically, but was helpless in his grip. Deliberately, he searched her person until he found the other gun and tossed that, also, across the room—found the vial of poison and smashed it.

Pinioned defenselessly against his powerful chest, Nita still fought on, but without strength, without hope. His face pressed toward hers—and across the room a windowpane broke crashingly inward! A man's voice called out clearly—a voice she knew—and loved!

"Turn around Satan, and take it!" It was Richard Wentworth.

Satan whirled, Nita held as a shield before him. His voice ripped out hoarsely. "Spring the trap, men!"

Wentworth was dropping to the floor inside the room. He held a heavy automatic in each fist.

"Shoot, Dick!" Nita cried. "There are a dozen men here to kill you! Shoot!"

Satan's right arm was clasped about her breasts, binding her arms to her side. She could feel his swift movements as he pulled out a weapon hidden somewhere in the scarlet suit. She saw Wentworth's heavy automatic raise, and smiled into his eyes. Powder flame darted toward her. The blast of the .45 caliber gun smashed against her eardrums. Satan's arm was torn away from her, and she dropped to her hands and knees upon the floor.

Behind her, she heard Satan's voice lift in a wild, hoarse scream of pain. Then the door clapped shut and the voice went on shouting—but *orders* now, clean-cut and incisive. In two long bounds, Wentworth was beside her, had thrown his arms around her. He must protect her!

"Out the window, Nita," he gasped. "I didn't hurt you?"

Nita staggered to her feet "I... I don't know. No, of course not, Dick. You shot his arm?"

Wentworth did not answer. He had swung her in his arms and crossed the room in long bounds, thrust her out through the window. Behind him, there was a series of muffled explosions.

"The death-dust!" he gasped. "I have only one gas mask and I've got to stay to finish that beast! Out that window!"

Wentworth was climbing out the window also. He peered back into the basement room in which Nita had been held prisoner, a hard, anxious glitter in his eyes. Swirling white dust blurred the lights, made iridescent gleams in the air. Abruptly, the door across the room *whanged* open and a rush of men poured through, Satan in their midst. Masks covered their faces; guns were in their hands.

Wentworth began shooting, but not at the men themselves. Water and steam pipes ran across the ceiling of the basement room, and it was at those Wentworth threw his bullets. The masks would save the men from the whirling white death-dust, but against the acid it would create, they had no protection! Three times Wentworth fired, and two streams of water gushed from water pipes. A white rush of steam geysered across the ceiling. The men... *screamed!*

INSTANTLY WENTWORTH was on his feet and, an arm around Nita, he whirled her along the stone wall of the house and toward the door. If Satan escaped that other trap, Wentworth's guns would be ready.

"Oh, Dick!" she whispered. "I thought you had died in that gas-main explosion. But I was sure you couldn't follow me. I hoped you couldn't. They were planning to trap you here. I didn't know how—"

"I came faster than they expected," Wentworth said grimly. "I was knocked out by that gas blast, but luckily I wasn't in the tunnels themselves. Jackson lost your signals. Jenkyns lost them, too, after a while, but Leary managed to stick to your trail. He called Jenkyns, and so I knew the neighborhood to come to. Leary and I worked out a triangulation and...."

Satan's scarlet figure plunged out of the basement door. Screams tore out hoarsely from beneath his mask, and he was plucking at his clothing, inside which the acid was eating into his body.

"At the throat, Dick!" Nita whispered.

Wentworth fired once, and Satan was hammered back against the stone wall. Crimson spread down and dimmed the glittering fire of his scarlet suit, then he slumped to the ground. Wentworth strode fiercely forward, guns ready, but there was no need of them. With a single, swift movement, he ripped the mask from the head... and Nita cried out in horror. Under that mask, the acid had been at work. Eyes, nose and cheeks were gone.

Grim-mouthed, Wentworth bent above the horror and ground upon the forehead the seal of the Spider.

"Leary is waiting nearby," Wentworth said, "and I have an appointment at noon to award some medals to Major Dow and Modoc O'Malley for catching Satan!"

His arm around Nita, he walked slowly toward the street.

"Mr. Wentworth," a man spoke just behind him. "Don't attempt to draw a gun."

Wentworth whirled about and looked into the leveled revolver of Donald Leary!

"I came too late to see you put your seal on Satan over there," he went on, a tremor in his voice, "but that won't be necessary. The bullets in his body will match with the guns under your arms. I'll have to trouble you for them."

Nita strode forward. "You ingrate!" she snapped. "It was the Spider that put his seal upon Satan. He came in at the last moment to save us."

"Then the guns won't prove a thing," Leary said grimly.

Wentworth put his hand on Nita's shoulder and drew her back. "Against Leary, darling," he said, "I am defenseless. If it had not been for him, I would never have found you here."

WENTWORTH WATCHED Leary with eyes that were alert and ready. But there was only one means by which he could overcome Leary. He could snatch out his guns and shoot, perhaps in time.

Slowly, Wentworth drew the guns from his holsters, and there was a wild urgency within him. One man stood between him and liberty. The moment he was definitely identified as the Spider, there would be a hundred cases of murder filed against him. He could never escape.

Wentworth tossed the guns on the ground, and something like a shudder ran over him. He had never shot down an innocent man.

"I knew what you were trying to do, Leary," he said. "You're welcome to those guns. They won't prove anything, even though you have the blood tests to back them up. They couldn't match with bullets the Spider fired, could they?"

Leary said, "Back up, five paces."

"I thought for a while," Wentworth said calmly, "that you were one of Satan's men. I guessed that you were in the employ of Modoc O'Malley, and you seemed to know so much about the possible plans of the men of Satan. You got those tips from O'Malley, didn't you?"

Leary was picking up the guns warily. "What difference does that make?"

"He could also," Wentworth pointed out, "phone an anonymous tip to Major Dow, after having said for weeks that Samuel Marco and the Communists were plotting against the country. Major Dow went to stop Marco and—listen to this—Marco didn't open fire! The firing was done by two men Dow thought were Marco's henchmen—but weren't. They were men put there by Satan. Then Satan killed both those men and wounded Dow—through the leg so that suspicion would fall on him." He nodded.

"Modoc O'Malley framed a story of having been shot by thugs on the street. Why, if he had so many detectives, weren't any there to defend him, Leary?"

Leary stared at Wentworth. "Hell, you're trying to say that O'Malley is Satan? That's crazy. A fine man like O'Malley."

Nita laughed bitterly. "You're saying Richard Wentworth is the Spider. And Richard Wentworth has been pretty kind to you, Mr. Leary!"

"O'Malley couldn't be Satan," Leary whispered. "He *couldn't* be! Why, if he was… he'd be a damned hypocrite!"

"That's a mild word for what really is, Leary," Wentworth said quietly. "Surely, knowing O'Malley as well as you do, you should be able to remember some distinguishing mark, or…."

"Yes," Leary said flatly, "there was a triangular scar on the palm of his left hand. If you're right… No tricks! I warn you, I'll shoot! You walk with me. Make a wide circle and put your back up against the wall of that house. You, too, Miss van Sloan!"

Wentworth obeyed and presently, hands lifted against the wall, beside Nita, he stood and watched. Leary squatted beside the body of Satan and fumbled with his hand. Then Leary threw a quick glance down at it, jumped to his feet.

"Good God!" he cried. "It *is* O'Malley! Why, damn him, he's the one who promised me he'd make me commissioner of the police if I caught the Spider! The dirty, murdering scoundrel! Pretending to want a clean city and killing innocent men and women to fill his own pockets. While you, Mr. Wentworth, preach death to the criminal and are kind. Patricia told me. I… Thank God you killed him, Mr. Wentworth!"

Wentworth said softly, "It was the Spider who killed him."

Leary stared at Wentworth, then looked down at the two guns he held in his left hand, the guns that could send Wentworth to the electric chair.

A small, stiff smile had come to Leary's lips, and now he stepped toward Wentworth. He held out the two guns he had taken.

148

"You're right," he said slowly, "it was the Spider who killed him... and a damned good job it was, too!"

POPULAR HERO PULPS AVAILABLE NOW:

ACE G-MAN
❑ #1: The Suicide Squad Reports for Death $14.95

CAPTAIN COMBAT
❑ #1: The Sky Beast of Berlin $13.95
❑ #2: Red Wings For the Blood Battalion $13.95
❑ #3: Low Ceiling For Nazi Hell Hawks $13.95

OPERATOR 5
❑ #1: The Masked Invasion $13.95
❑ #2: The Invisible Empire $13.95
❑ #3: The Yellow Scourge $13.95
❑ #4: The Melting Death $13.95
❑ #5: Cavern of the Damned $13.95
❑ #6: Master of Broken Men $13.95
❑ #7: Invasion of the Dark Legions $13.95
❑ #8: The Green Death Mists $13.95
❑ #9: Legions of Starvation $13.95
❑ #10: The Red Invader $13.95
❑ #11: The League of War-Monsters $13.95
❑ #12: The Army of the Dead $13.95
❑ #13: March of the Flame Marauders $13.95
❑ #14: Blood Reign of the Dictator $13.95
❑ #15: Invasion of the Yellow Warlords $13.95
❑ #16: Legions of the Death Master $13.95
❑ #17: Hosts of the Flaming Death $13.95
❑ #18: Invasion of the Crimson Death Cult $13.95
❑ #19: Attack of the Blizzard Men $13.95
❑ #20: Scourge of the Invisible Death $13.95
❑ #21: Raiders of the Red Death $13.95
❑ #22: War-Dogs of the Green Destroyer $13.95
❑ #23: Rockets From Hell $13.95
❑ #24: War-Masters from the Orient $13.95
❑ #25: Crime's Reign of Terror $13.95
❑ #26: Death's Ragged Army $13.95
❑ #27: Patriots' Death Battalion $13.95
❑ #28: The Bloody Forty-five Days $13.95
❑ #29: America's Plague Battalions $13.95
❑ #30: Liberty's Suicide Legions $13.95
❑ #31: Siege of the Thousand Patriots $13.95
❑ #32: Patriots' Death March $14.95

DUSTY AYRES AND HIS BATTLE BIRDS
❑ #1: Black Lightning! $13.95
❑ #2: Crimson Doom $13.95
❑ #3: The Purple Tornado $13.95
❑ #4: The Screaming Eye $13.95
❑ #5: The Green Thunderbolt $13.95
❑ #6: The Red Destroyer $13.95
❑ #7: The White Death $13.95
❑ #8: The Black Avenger $13.95
❑ #9: The Silver Typhoon $13.95
❑ #10: The Troposphere F-S $13.95
❑ #11: The Blue Cyclone $13.95
❑ #12: The Tesla Raiders $13.95

MAVERICKS
❑ #1: Five Against the Law $12.95
❑ #2: Mesquite Manhunters $12.95
❑ #3: Bait for the Lobo Pack $12.95
❑ #4: Doc Grimson's Outlaw Posse $12.95
❑ #5: Charlie Parr's Gunsmoke Cure $12.95

THE MYSTERIOUS WU FANG
❑ #1: The Case of the Six Coffins $12.95
❑ #2: The Case of the Scarlet Feather $12.95
❑ #3: The Case of the Yellow Mask $12.95
❑ #4: The Case of the Suicide Tomb $12.95
❑ #5: The Case of the Green Death $12.95
❑ #6: The Case of the Black Lotus $12.95
❑ #7: The Case of the Hidden Scourge $12.95

THE SECRET 6
❑ #1: The Red Shadow $13.95
❑ #2: House of Walking Corpses $13.95
❑ #3: The Monster Murders $13.95
❑ #4: The Golden Alligator $13.95

CAPTAIN ZERO
❑ #1: City of Deadly Sleep $13.95
❑ #2: The Mark of Zero! $13.95
❑ #3: The Golden Murder Syndicate $13.95